THE OWL
AND
THE GOOSE ON THE GRAVE

Books by John Hawkes

The Cannibal (1949)
The Bettle Leg (1951)
The Goose on the Grave AND *The Owl* (1954)
The Lime Twig (1961)
Second Skin (1964)
The Innocent Party: Four Short Plays (1966)
Lunar Landscapes: Stories & Short Novels 1949–1963 (1969)
The Blood Oranges (1971)
Death, Sleep & The Traveler (1974)
Travesty (1976)
The Passion Artist (1979)
Virginie, Her Two Loves (1982)
Humors of Blood and Skin (1984)
Innocence in Extremis (1985)
Adventures in the Alaskan Skin Trade (1985)
Whistlejacket (1988)
Sweet William: A Memoir of Old Horse (1993)

JOHN HAWKES

The Owl

AND

The Goose on the Grave

Two Short Novels

SUN &
MOON

CLASSICS

67

LOS ANGELES
SUN & MOON PRESS
1994

Sun & Moon Press
A Program of The Contemporary Arts Educational Project, Inc.
a nonprofit corporation
6026 Wilshire Boulevard, Los Angeles, California 90036

This edition first published in paperback in 1994 by Sun & Moon Press
10 9 8 7 6 5 4 3 2 1
FIRST SUN & MOON EDITION
©1954 by John Hawkes
Reprinted by arrangement with New Directions
Publishing Corporation
Biographical information ©1994 Sun & Moon Press

This book was made possible, in part, through an operational grant from
the Andrew W. Mellon Foundation, and through contributions to
The Contemporary Arts Educational Project, Inc.,
a nonprofit corporation

Cover: Tommaso Lisanti, *Stream (Corrente)*, 1984
Design: Katie Messborn
Typography: Guy Bennett

LIBRARY OF CONGRESS CATALOGING IN PUBLICATION DATA
Hawkes, John
The Owl and The Goose on the Grave
p. cm (Sun & Moon Classics: 67)
ISBN: 1-55713-194-5
I. Title. II. Series.
811'.54—dc20

Printed in the United States of America on acid-free paper.

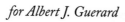

for Albert J. Guerard

Contents

The Owl

"Him?

Think not of him for your daughter, Signore, nor for her sister either. There will be none for him. Not him. He has taken his gallows, the noose and knot, to marry."

The fathers of Sasso Fetore, their chins in hand, let me by and stuffed away the dowries, squinting at the shadow of the tall lady at my side. Though I was named Il Gufo, the owl, I was tall as she. One by one they deliberated, and well they might, for Sasso Fetore had few left who could walk on the cold stone in the morning without clutching their knees, curling their toes, bending their bare narrow backs, who could wake and anticipate the cry of guai! on the cold air. Few enviable as I. If a father had once seen Il Gufo, sucked in his breath when I was pointed out to him, he might climb again to the fortress for another look, alone. Theirs were

the wobbling legs and, at the last minute rubbing tobacco under their lips and turning to flee, they had no
word for the hangman. Not one had thought to put his
daughter's hand into mine or expected mine to fall on
hers. Now they were tempted.

But with each new day the old fathers of Sasso Fetore
returned to the field, pressing here and there the suit of a
Teresa, Lucia, Antonina, Ginevra. The woman Antonina
accompanied her father and if his task, hasty, catholic,
were not impossible, she made it easier. Even when passing the bodies of the foot soldiers, blackened chimney
boys, collected in the ravines like thin logs with blackened shields or visors turned up to the weather, they de-
vised second best plans for making husband of the prisoner held captive in the hangman's fortress. And at the
time when light rain or storm quickly darked the fortress any hour, my ward Pucento was begging for a wife.

The prisoner, delivered into altitude where there was
time and silence to devour him, was the hangman's. The
fortress which kept him safe was cleft in two parts on
the pinnacle of the city, high tower and low tower, and
from either battlement there was an iron-edged view of
the world, its cliff, the tilted slopes at the bottom, the
sunrise and sunset, and, not so far off, the border itself of
a definite black and white. To the east it was possible to
find a thin white horizon, the sea. If any in Sasso Fetore
saw out there a Venetian sail, they pretended it was a
dream.

The fortress was property willed to Sasso Fetore's
hangman; his also the road winding from the valley, the

produce of the fair set up summers at the foot of the mountain, the remains of the monastery and Campo Santo, and the barrenness of the wasted descents below covered with briar and rose campions. To the hangman went the souls of death's peasants, to him were bonded the lineage of a few artisans and not least the clarity of such a high place, a long firm line of rule. If there was decay, it was only in the walls falling away from proclamations hundreds of years old, still readable, still clear and binding.

The sun reached the mountain first and finally the valley. Each morning I waited for the light, and from the high tower, back to the steady winds, I watched the border until I saw the white skeletons of horses and men with hanging heads, the white bones of the legs sinking into the sand, the pistols swinging against pumiced hip bones. An order kept them ever moving around the mountain clock.

"Mi scusi, Hangman," the first deputy would shout, "it is time to assemble!"

Leaving, taking another good breath as I turned, my boot might kick a stone from the battlement and down it would fall until I heard it land with a breaking of shells in one of the rook's nests that littered the golden vertical cuts of the cliff. My boots were the heaviest of all, black, laced under the knee. The birds made no sound but suffered these accidents in silence as if natural. The cloud formations over Sasso Fetore were consistent of color, large and geometric, the clear head of a Roman heaven.

By a decree dating to the Council of Bishops and

Gaolers, the heart of the hangman's escutcheon burst and became an owl: with wisdom, horns, and field rodent half-destroyed, hardly visible under the talons. The bird, the scholar with his hunger clamped exactingly to the rudimental prey, peered from his shield tacit, powerful, bits of ruff and gut caught to his savage bill. The owl. And the hangmen, as they came down the inviolable line, sat or hooked the demanding winged beasts upon their necks and shoulders, lordly claws digging into lordly men, and assumed rule to the archaic slow drumming of the nocturnal thick wings against their ears, bearing instantaneously the pain of authority injected directly into their blood streams, as the owl clutched and hooted of old upon the darkened tree tops.

The owl kept watch on peasant and prefect alike. He sat erect, taking keen sanctuary among the stones of the campanile, unmoved while slitting the thin stomach of some gray animal with his beak or dusting with his low matted feathers our rubrics. On a cold throne, twisted branch, he kept a mute, tenacious, arbitrary peace, fit with little exercise, thirsting quietly for the scrap of ligament or skin needed to keep him cloaked above the city another hundred years. He had a foul breath, a deadly hold, and was quick; his eyes, and the trembling in the short armour feathers, the beak that when sated remained locked, were for the cold law and sermon that came out of the forest to make the husbandman quake. To some he brought this surety of judgment and the vision, challenging, of the broken neck. I am speaking of myself, Il Gufo.

To the hangman also went a senatorial apartment and a donkey. Faggots for the cold of winter were supplied on the hunched back of a creature, Monco, who had in his youth fallen from a parapet of the fortress and survived.

They in Sasso Fetore said that I rubbed soot on my face before sleep, that I possessed a lock of every hanged man's hair, that I confessed once a year to a Jesuit exiled from the Holy See, and that I collected about me varieties of stinging insects. None of this: my walls, ceilings, and stairwells were painted often with a white chalk, fresh and sharp as bone, and not a shadow went undetected. The sun was urged down the spires of the scaffold. But the old men of Sasso Fetore needed to talk of their hangman.

Up and down the cleared streets they went, peering overhead lest the bough break, spoke of young women in wait at home, every day combing their hair in a different style, each villa, town house, hut become an urgent convent. Most, like Antonina, were mistresses of bridal chests filled with seven years' accumulation of lace and white bodices, linen, and trinkets that were bolted from the rain. Their fathers plied for them by day, toured the countryside, down on the rocks they beat their hands under the prison windows. The girls were not merely virgin, those unseen propagated a sense of the timelessness of denial, of death hung rocking around and around on the broken-spoked wheel atop a pole. Little Ginevra was kept at home; Antonina, with compressed jaws, came to see for herself the smoke rising from the mass, the even rows of old women paddling their wash, the air of vigil and continuance over the bridled province.

"He hangs them until dead. Will we have a race of executioners, Signore? Let her be still."

However, they turned to stare, to speculate on Il Gufo with or without hopes of conjugation even though the custom of ribaldry and carousing during the season of the summer fair fell more and more into disuse. The men now alive, remaining, had not often seen me in a black hood and waited for the sight.

Storms came from the prohibited east of the ocean. Green and sudden and, sometimes mixed with snow, they battered first the fortress, tearing the bartizans, dislodging and rolling into the air the rooks incapable of opening their wings. For kilometers the rose campions were pierced under the hail and the vineyards bodingly destroyed. Rain scrubbed the high cobblestones, made the straw roofs swell and doors swell, imprisoning Sasso Fetore behind the thickened jambs. Nowhere could a man walk without seeing through the rain the city's virginal design, the plan of its builders: the sheer blackness of stone intended to resist and put tooth to the howl and sluice of water, intact as it was, echoing, beset with the constant fall of the rain, unviolated and dark as in the Holy Day curfew of the year twelve hundred. No storm could dislodge those early grimly smelted chains but rather gave the city its victory in its architecture fixed, steeply pitched, weatherbeaten. Not a bolt rang. As a prosecuted law with the ashes of suffering and memory carried off on the wind, Sasso Fetore was a judgment passed upon the lava, long out of date, was the more intolerant and severe. Only the absolute wheel is known, old as it is, and I looked for the first exacting laws in the archaic, listened for the skidding of an obsolete machine on the narrow driving streets.

"He shall be dead, by means described hereafter, on the first sunless day to come, and his soul shall be said to exist no more." The census of Sasso Fetore was set with the great seal of depuration—jugglers, actors, lame soldiers, all condemned and hanged.

The snow, falling morning and night upon the head and arms of the Donna, inevitably ended in an hour brighter than any season's and one, two, but no more, children and perhaps my ward Pucento slid down the slopes on their bare haunches. Hatless, without sweaters, one or three black merrymakers scaled down the white field kicking against the snow, careful to make no noise, each figure far apart and a speck black as a devil's finger. Then Signor Barabo, Antonina's father, would climb into the town, up the narrow street with his brief under his arm and head bent as if looking for a drop of blood on the snow. He stopped to read every proclamation again. He had some divination into the past, for he knew that a hanged man's legs were bound at the ankles, that once the body is on the rope it is at the executioner's disposal to hang it as long as he wished, a week or a day. And while thinking of this ritual, Signor Barabo thought at the same time of the ritual in which the groom and groomsmen were about to fall upon his Antonina, corset, mantilla, and all.

The road up the valley was almost impassable in the snow. A thin fox, the old man might traverse it but the way was unbroken as if the forbidden horizon of the sea had crept during the night to our walls and pickets. My donkey's hoofs split in winter, still I drove him each day under the seven foot arches of Sasso Fetore burdened with a saddle built of wood and iron and bound to him by a girth that froze and cut the belly. The tips of the donkey's ears were cut through and a small rusted bell permanently fixed to each that jangled to his uneven gait and high station. Astride him early in the cold and short-breathed brilliant morning—the pinnacle of Sasso Fetore was like a crag summoned from the Alpine assizes—I sometimes heard the prefect's voice piping our drawn streets: "Permesso. Countrymen, good morning!" I would pull sharply on the bridle.

In Sasso Fetore all but the prefect welcomed the communication of interdicts whether cried or posted, "Blaspheme no more. Il Gufo." During the rain, or after one of the determined snowfalls, this injunction met the eye of every man and boy and was obeyed. The fox was traditionally the blasphemer, and the white length of the idle valley road was littered with the red carcass trapped in winter by a few terrified children blowing on their fingers. My ward Pucento cut the tail off close as he could. I saw Signor Barabo cover the fox hastily with snow. A dead fox meant another wedless day.

Signor Barabo forever carried with him some item intimate to the nuptial, the garter, the soldi the bride tucks against her bosom, some aphrodisiac trinket he had spirited from Antonina's seven year store. One of the articles often in his possession was the private purse she carried under her skirts. And this he displayed under the priest's window as if a lucky impregnation might come between the secular nectary and the sacred. Signor Barabo's heart, consciousness, and ambition ended in an appendage that housed the kidney and overhung his groin like a tapir's snout—blind sack he lightly rubbed while discoursing and guardedly measuring the passers-by. He had a large flap hanging from the shoulder under cover of his coat. On winter evenings when his old wife massaged it with liniment, he struck her and, enraged, leaned over again so that the deformity rose up with uncanny liveliness to be oiled. Outside he was a peasant, inside a fish whose concealed pouches could inflate to considerable size until he groaned in his own monstrous dimensions.

"My Antonina, my daughter Antonina, will be ready to take her husband immediately after the Pentecost."

Antonina was a woman with a narrow girdle and face the soft color of an olive. It gave me the same strong feeling of satisfaction to see her as it did to spy my ward Pucento falling about in the snow, the western gradation of white marred by the far-off kicking and helpless salutes of his lengthy arms and legs, an autonomous and senseless play before the afternoon closed to the rising of the wind. It pleased me to watch him attempting to steady himself, the black straw on his head rolling across the snow field, one at least from whom the owl could snatch a river fish without trouble, so valueless was he.

Idyllic his thin trunk, woman's voice, his pranks in which he exposed his shivery loins unwittingly to the power around him. Pucento as my ward remained to hurtle himself against Sasso Fetore's grave unrestored stones, a jest of flesh, angular, laughing, incompetent.

"Pucento," early in the morning I leaned over his bed, "Pucento," I said until he opened his eyes. And, but a moment awake, flat on his back and face to face with Il Gufo, he would try to answer, fall to twisting from side to side, clutching at the gray shirt he slept in and grimacing. He little thought of jesting if I caught him with the dream still on his fingertips and if I broke in upon his disarray and refuge. "Buon giorno, Pucento." As soon as I moved, he lapsed into sleep again. Waking later, he his own medium, he would bolt for the cold street shouting, "Faggots, faggots!" heels skipping high as his knee and wailing as if the wood might crawl to him at a slow moving pace.

The parochial owl hooted and Pucento made a good deal of noise before he thought better. At night he sat in front of the wintry red brazier and I put him to work kneading my virgin rope coils. He ate cheese cut from a large white tub. The owl stood above us like a thick-chested, legless, disciplined commandant facing, between torn forests, a ragged enemy of Austerlitz.

I watched the coming of dark from the high tower. Sasso Fetore, its roofs sharply crumpled and pitted below me, grew dark but never completely invisible, always some fragment of thatch or colored glass withstanding the night. There was only part shelter in the tower; I stood with my shoulders hidden in the damp and one fist and my face raised, exposed to the rush of air, the long fall away to the villas and water wheel lost below—that curious feeling in the fortress of half human, half mildew of history, a precarious high post with the open night in front and a wet niche in the stones behind. I gripped one of the cornices. And the moon passed, small, cold, flying between the dead trees. The ordeal of older tribunals, the plagues that attended the newborn and the roof of black stoop-shouldered angels that awaited them, the fiber and the crack of the ferrule amongst the population, these I thought of in the evening when my boot heel ground under a bit of fortress rock scum.

Down, in the dark, the peasants were eating their macaroni, flat bread, and a paste made of sheep gut. On each wooden table was a liter flask; the wine was new as sap. It was as if I saw them all, corselet, benches, arms and legs, Garibaldis burning in a cold and windy piazza, so certainly were they in the outer and lower spaces, peaceful. And behind the huts, near the mouth of the cave marked by a white statue of the Donna on a pedestal, lay Sasso Fetore's forests, barbed and stripped to order. Here the female owl scratched at her blue egg with a diamond.

"*Signore. He sleeps in black sheets. Black straw lies in his stable. I would not give him my daughter—no, Master—not even if he does eat, I've heard said, the pulp of freshly crushed deer antlers. Cross yourself, Signore. Take my advice.*"

Like oxmen huddled around a milk cart in a dry rut, they had their opinions. But whether the issue that gave shape to the head and bulged the eyes was the catechism, the death of a prized boar, or a remark about little Ginevra's beauty, the old men soaked their hands in warmed oil and all their thoughts and feelings, the very grayness of hair, vanished when the hangman put on his black cape.

It was the prefect who kept the streets picked clean. I could urge my donkey to a gallop until his shoulder blades rubbed and the bells tinkled unnaturally at the tips of his long white ears, and from one end of Sasso Fetore to the other I could see dry gutters, not a dead raven or a cat, no new piling of dung, and down below the captive sewerage. The small man, fastidious only in size and weight, scourged the lice; short, thin, his bones so many that they formed, instead of a skeleton, a mesh. Across his chest were belted two thin straps pulled to the last hole. The prefect inspected cupboard and water closet, descended into foundations hunting for ripened curd, wielding his torch and four-headed pike. His badge bore the wolves at the dugs, his brief epaulettes, his black hair hewn to the narrow side, and he obeyed, though not without pinching his little lip until it became white. He lived alone below the fortress within shouting distance of the dungeon, sleeping on a cot like a field commander. Martial drum and thin trunks of plants were hung about the walls and obscured the windows.

Of all the prefect's belongings, only his stately ganders seemed descended from Sasso Fetore's own lofty impartiality. His four red-eyed birds, though they had little to eat, covered the countryside in good regiment, their tense hungry step marching over sand, ashes, trampling the rose campions. No girl could drive these white creatures in such formation, and one behind the other, making no noise, they hunted small game and insects. To see them in single file atop the fortress—even I looked up. Or below, in the ravines, winding their way among the dead, always white, sharp-billed, not so beautiful that they would keep from scavenging. Sometimes only the necks were visible, long white necks that might be broken in a dozen places; fierceness and starvation were evident in the ganders' windpipes unreasonably stretched in God's dark and genic pillory. The fowl survived, now holding their flat honed bills high asway against the horizon. The four of them, Sasso Fetore's flock, never emitted the shrill crabbing sounds of their species but appeared on the steep slippery cobblestones in silence, checking themselves, and it was with precision, quickly, that they pecked anyone who crossed their path, thrust forward the snowy Netherlandish throats like serpents. Sometimes I tempted them with my fingers, but they did not bite and continued their marching.

Perhaps Sasso Fetore was most lofty when no one was in sight, when the owl was at his instruction and outside the ganders were poised, making little headway against the sunset, the blue wind ruffling their single file, when the rope swaying from the tall lady dangled idly like a ship cable in the middle of the voyage, and the province, sloping upward, was burnished red and gold, like a Florentine coin, before night. Faintly, in his knotty ears, the donkey's bells would jangle. And the fortress with its rocky view showed its temporary darkling life of lanterns. "Buona notte, Hangman. Good shelter," whispered the last to leave the streets. The clapper hung silent in the campanile, while it was still day, the curfew formidable over sagging bellies, over the aged coveting their anchovies in the dark, out of sight. I looked up, down, Sasso Fetore held the spirit, the law of the swift leg, stones reddening above a country that had no marsh.

At the last moment, before the windy collapse of the day—swiftly it deserted, sinking to another meridian— I myself took the road down toward the ravines and stakes of shriveling berries, keeping to the center of the way, holding firmly the donkey's jaw. A little dust rose some feet behind. And from the cliff, huddled under the balistraria far overhead, I might hear old men playing the viola da gamba, their black coats sawing musically to the left and right in the very position of skirmishers.

Many ravines were empty, offering at most a bit of crackling skin cast off from the snake, a dark spot where moisture was working up from the center of the earth; but in others sat the foot fighters who would run no more, the burned bodies listing into the sand. I rode on the edge of these pits and then through them. I counted the backs of the heads. I looked at them lying upon the earth like assassinated sheep. The remains of a water-cooled cannon were driven deep into the sand. The trenches were filled with letters, in the moonlight I looked at them, letters dropped during the summer and again the next summer on the faces of the dead. The letters were strewn upon the cinders and some had been torn open by animals. And some stuck to my boot heel. I pulled the donkey after me and could not control where he stepped.

The dead were lieges to Sasso Fetore's hangman, a chary parliament with which he met at dusk, having no voices to raise and unable to tell which limbs were lost or which ribs had been staved in the process of death's accomplishment, what weight of marrow and gut given. The numbers I stumbled on, pitifully small, did accrue in some historic calculation, out of their tangle raising an arithmetic council that gave more body to their subservience than the hair, cloth, and tissue withering. I climbed through the ashes hearing my foot turn over a trench knife or wooden shoe; and the contortions, the shrinking about the knees, the unexpected oddments I found poking in the soot, in a Roman fire, were symmetrical, ordered, suitable as the leaning masts topped by slowly turning wheels that were implanted—some signaling device, not monument—in their midst.

It was here I thought of Antonina going to her bed.

Night. I was a lonely rider who urged his donkey into an overheated aged canter on the lesser slopes, and fast even as we returned up the mountain, the road became straight and high, bleak with hoarfrost. My boots, protecting as jambeaux, rubbed his hide back near the tender joining of haunches, the spurs rang. Behind I was followed by speechless adventure, the impersonal ganders. Below, the foot soldiers must wait another inspection, thoughtlessly camped in the hollows where the summer fairs were pitched. Balcony, turret, cloister, arcade, the stones immobile in tempest, all silent and austere, the city descended a few hundred meters and stopped, formidable even to me. A city through the center of which grappled the prefect's four hooks, a place part chalet, part slaughterhouse, with scrollwork upon the gables and brass crowns upon the chimneys, a province whose wooden coffins were lined with porcelain, whose garrets were filled with ransacked portraits of dignitaries and half-eaten goose. Without mass violence, Sassa Fetore was still unmerciful, it was visible in the moonlight, purposeful as the avalanche of rock and snow. Here in the cellars and under roofs far as the boundary, the old men slept in their stockings and the others, confident wives, warmed wedding bands in their armpits. Politically, historically, Sasso Fetore was an eternal Sabbath.

Using flint, iron, and tinder, I struck a flame to the candle at the base of the white statue of the Donna to whom was attributed tolerable beauty and humility and who was thought to destroy dreams. Perhaps to her could be laid the spirit of black and white in the peasant, that suited their soft flesh in both valediction and penalty. Surely the Donna made the scaffold majestic. Week after week of Sabbaths attested to this, when the regimen set down for the citizens was not perfectly autonomous and in the blue night some worshipped object was accountable to the spirit, or the spirit for a moment was awed in some simple fashion; when the law gave bony strength to the lover of Donna and legend. The character and the code, right upon right, crashed into the pale heart when the culprit hanged, her prayers for him so soft as hardly to be heard. She saved none—salvation not being to the purpose—yet, like the virgins, stood off with low head and waited for movement from him bound on the gibbet. Her statue was placed before the cave near the forest and owl's tree.

And the prisoner: perhaps he too had his Donna or some lady to accompany him to captivity. Perhaps he too had his fragile witness in another language and blessed in that outlandish tongue. And if so, perhaps she lent him an untouchable comfort in the cell, peace, his angelo keeping him quiet as he kissed her feet or paid whatever was her homage. Perhaps she assured him of clemency and calmed him. But I would think not.

Guai! Guai!

The sound made my ward Pucento pull his hands and wince about the eyes and mouth. It was Pucento who started the rumor that I would hang him immediately after the Pentecost. How could he know the day!

Several paths led to the fortress. The approaches to the prison that appeared so inaccessible from the slopes below or from the boundaries—on some mornings the patrol raised their skeletal hands—were ready, easy, and at one turning there was even an abandoned pump as if it was here that visitors were expected to drag their mounts, here that they should naturally stop to drink, being able to climb little further. All men wanted to reach quickly, to see for themselves, either the high tower or the low, bloodying their fingers if necessary, sparing not their heart valves or horse. At a bend in the high path there were loose stones that, along with nature's debris deposited in the ruin, fell down upon the rooks. Antonina let her hair drape against the rotted pump the wood of which concealed in its grain a hundred eyes; the ganders favored the low path with their rhythmic scuttling, their search for food out of the rocky air. There was a place in the middle path, steepest and most direct way to the fortification, where from an irregular hole in the rock no larger than three fingers flowed a constant trickle of water, always to be found stirring, always seeping down, draining, from the dungeons—on the brightest of days and though it had not rained for weeks. It was water they said that cooled the ardor.

In the morning, early, the unshaved prefect climbed to the prisoner with unusual speed, as if to put to his lips the treacherous and unruly ram's horn. Bloodshot, hurrying when it was not yet his hour to come to the streets, he avoided my eye, a nightmare still fresh in his head, and as he passed he covered his eye nearest me with the glove that pinched the fingers and left the wrist bare, hardly saluting, carrying his water quickly along in a rat's sack. And already the prisoner studied the lines in his hands and picked at his incomprehensible tin insignia, the badge of those about to die in public.

And still Signor Barabo tried to speak to the prisoner. He petitioned to husband him. He asked for his name. Promising him—sure of my pardon—consigning his very procreative parts to this daughter or that and joining him to his otherwise fruitless family. And Signor Barabo was not alone. The men, oldest of all, with lids falling away from canine eyes, with clay pipes wrapped around their fingers, could be seen every day dusting, dusting the studs, the iron, the boot toes, a long and tenuous bell pull, hook-backed and hard at work polishing the war horse. They uncorked bottles of spumante. The prefect talked; and in the excitement some suppliant thought to smear the face of the Donna with blood. There was more spumante.

I, hangman of Sasso Fetore, prepared in another manner to give them a spectacle that would bring a laugh, a cry, and an upsurge even from my confessor, the Jesuit.

I washed down the scaffolding brought from the seventh hill.

I, hangman of Sasso Fetore, set in motion the proceedings that drew ledgers from their vaults and inkpots to the oak table, pushing the rafters, the spokes, the axle cold and thick with bear grease, touching these ancient parts in the law's carriage house—and through the city I had justice dragged on a hundred wheels roped to the distended body.

I went to see if they also were ready.

"But he has a fine stand, has he not?" The other, bowing his head, answered, *"He has, Signore."*

And the old man, muttering to himself, would set

off as if to settle the matter immediately, jogging his proposals and senility, muttering in Sasso Fetore's pantomime, smiling down the hill and moving his lips.

The Prisoner Comes

"Permetta che le presenti mia figlia. Permetta che le presenti mia figlia Antonina."

It was the feeling in Sasso Fetore that after this introduction, she—be she Teresa or Antonina—would say, "Quando potrò riverderla?" hiding hair and throat in a tight veil. During the warm weather they stood out on the rocks to watch, a young woman standing white as the Donna upon each stone below the cliff. The romantic gambados of all such as Signor Barabo—these aging courtiers—tempered the season, and the cockle cap, the red noses, turned to home greatly astir. The devil sat between Signor Barabo's shoulders and breathed heat down his neck. There was an air about Sasso Fetore—it was felt in the council, near the pump, or behind a stained glass—that one wretched mass of the sex was about to rise to the temptation.

What one of them did not expect to husband my prisoner?

Signora Barabo, with fiery arms, bathed her daughters in an alcove behind the farmhouse and the water ran from under the bristling swine, seeping across the yard from the bath: first little Ginevra and then Antonina, sparing neither, the shouts of the three women loud as slaves naked in their stockade. And not a word from Antonina when, accompanying her father, she carried pressed to her bosom a book from whose foot hung a flower, the Spinster's Needle, hardly moving under the clasp of her hand. In Sasso Fetore female fingers were powdered and ringed, were driven carelessly into dough or the common crush of blood apples, or took the axe to the pig.

It was at the time of the bath one day, when the owl also spit and picked his front, that my ward Pucento led a small column of soldiers, and amid them the prisoner, up the hangman's road. Pucento, the lictor, was well ahead and he was covered with the camouflage of torn coat, berretta, and dusty face. Pucento led his band past the girls' shifts drying on the barbed wire and forward to the steeper grade at the same moment Signora Barabo splashed Antonina from the bucket.

Pucento brandished the Roman fasces over his head. The bundle of straw and the scythe blade, arms of authority, these he kept thrusting left to right at the open road so that the rushes whistled and the blade hooked into the air. It was an instrument he might shake at the path of a fiend or rattle on the day of excoriation. Every few feet Pucento, still on his toes, suddenly crashed the jacketed axe head down upon the earth savagely as he could. I felt also his extravagance and I too the compulsion in his various steps. And as this small figure flexed his legs, his arms, even from the tower I could see that he was capable of cutting down the bush and huts as he passed.

The marchers that he led huddled together and tramped up the hill. They had been joined by one, two, members of that outermost patrol whose skulls were cavernous and whose muskets were covered with the bleach of bare collarbones. They walked heavily and clung to earth, often making a cordon out of their arms, knapsacks and blackened eyes; their greatcoats billowed and exposed the home-sewn sleeping shirts grained with lice. A rifle raised, I saw the black expulsion of shot and ball signaling their arrival.

They had come far. Still, close as they were to the end of the march, they crowded together, menacing their prisoner as if they could not bear to give him up.

A small child ran from a sty and threw grit into the midst of spiked boots, perspiration, and white lips. It was not long before those few figures old and bent out in the fields—accustomed as they were to till from light to dark without looking up from the furrow, so alike and so menial they could not be picked out from the clay and pinch of seed they attempted to sow—dropped their rakes. From several corners they hurried toward the road to stare after the band smelling of the capture. A foreign crow glided above them and watched for refuse. An old man shouted: "Come si chiama? Come si chiama?" excitedly, squeezing his hands. But if the prisoner understood, he dared not answer.

The wind tore to shreds the clouds about me, the taste of morning coffee and cognac was on my tongue, and so high on the fortress walk one could hardly imagine the burnished air and the moisture that lay in the beds of the bullocks at the foot of the valley. The rooks cowered in their nests. A spirit bottle had smashed on the stones in this deserted niche of the fortress and back and forth my boots ground the glass. It was a cold vigilant place. As I watched the progress of Pucento and his patrol, my mind measured off the fields like parallel rules: a hundred kilos would be reaped from that one, another hundred from that, in the middle field there was nothing except the grave of a peasant's small boy. The earth looked like the mud holes of rice flats, it stretched away only to provide a surface in which to hide excrement. On the eastern horizon, on the sea, a lone sail leaned down skirting the salt caps.

Then Pucento was nearer. They approached the gate that was proud only of its immunity after a past of doges, conservatories, learning and brotheldom—the Renaissance driven from our garrets and streets. The foot soldiers were close, the green skull caps, the rusted saber, the empty sacks. They disappeared into the arches and piazzas and the smell of burning twigs.

I was spared the sight of the women holding their bosoms to the window in welcome. Sasso Fetore gave them its unlatching of shutters, and they were followed by an old woman offering them a hot pullet. As the soldiers passed the coffin maker's shop, the old fellow poured a drop of spumante into the tin cup of each and tried to detain them.

"Where is your daughter, coffin maker?" growled one, taking his draught and flattening his boots on the stone.

"Inside, inside," was the quick answer. And, "Lucia! Come down, daughter!"

But they were gone and he drank a bit himself and sat upon the curb. Two children, dressed only in shirts, ran ahead and pounded on the doors, and their running feet sounded like a monkey clapping his hands. "La, la, la, la," were the exclamations within.

They went through the streets barely catching the pieces of bread and meat thrust at them, and they turned the corners all at once like a band no longer familiar with avenues and pedestrian courtesies, took large strides, men just come from marching in the snow. They were conscious of the weapons, the powder bags hanging to their bodies. They were poorly shaved, having cut at their faces out of doors and in cold water. But even those in Sasso Fetore had gray cheeks and oily hair, the marks of their Latin, circumspect temperament. Even Signor Barabo had inherited his weakness.

And men as well as women appeared at the windows to wave stockings or a wooden fork, wiping the wine from their lips and sleep from their eyes. "Che cosa, cosa?" whispered the very young until they were lifted to see. Pucento led his men upward through Sasso Fetore.

From the roofs below me rose a crematorial smoke which they had fanned to fire in the middle of their stone floors early that morning. The first awake had shaken the second in his blanket and then the third; with the confusion of dawn still upon them, they lifted dirty heads from their arms and a vocabulary humble as the sounds of animals was put to use again. All of them wanted to touch the prisoner who had not a moment been brought from the fields and ditches into the streets and bolted structures of Sasso Fetore, past the sagging figure of Signor Barabo himself gripping aloft a handkerchief and shouting: "Viva il prigioniero!"

From the absolute clarity of my vantage above—the wind was strong enough to prickle one's skin but leave the eyes starting from the head—I surveyed the slate roofs and beneath them those who hurried in anticipation through the morning.

The band emerged from the edge of the city and faltered a moment upon the plateau of the last back houses and overtoppled fountain, shouldering their arms before crossing the graveyard from which started the paths to the fortress. The eager crowd did not follow them from under the pitch of roofs and balconies, but the women and children went indoors again. Two old men tipped their heads together, held their arms up in excited tremor-boned salute, and went their separate ways, listening with their ears to the lock holes for what was to come.

Pucento thrust high the fasces and twisted them around and around in helpless signal, unable to move further, paralyzed with wine. The others pulled their coat collars over their mouths. But even paralyzed, Pucento's standstill was tormented with the sound of dogs leaping with torches in their jaws, his indecision comic and fearful as a clown's.

I leaned over the parapet. "Avanti!" I shouted, and at the command they rattled forward, striking their pennant staffs into the ruts. The owl hooted. The climbers in their bulky clothes tried to balance by clutching the blue and black scrub trees that twisted horizontally from the cliff. The hidden villagers sent up a low-lying olive smoke. Then I saw the prefect come out, finish his piece of dried pepper, hastily tuck his shirt into his trousers, and descend to meet the prisoner. He was short and wiry in the light. On his belt he carried a ring of keys and in his hand a pair of wrought iron pincers. He poked his sharp tongue against his cheek thoughtfully.

The ganders cut between the prefect and the prisoner. The birds, dragoons of the farmyard, precariously trod the sheer ledge, and continued unswervingly, keeping formation in unlikely crags and watches, pointing their sails, languid but regimented and stately despite webbed feet. White and silent was their propulsion. Between the prefect and Pucento, the ganders sailed with prohibitive bodies the shape of vindictive Flemish women's headgear wide and crackling beyond their backs.

I stood tall, shoulders hard against the round of the high tower, surveying the radii of earth not quite a maremma. And far, far off some low women beat their loaves upon an oxen's haunch. All about was the deceptive blue sky. In, out, to the chest and extended, I breathed deeply of the air the wind hath frozen in his belly. I hardly noticed the black tiles on the roofs directly below and did not know whether all were impassioned of the prisoner thinking he would escape the scaffold or, more likely, thinking I would hang him. But I did not concern myself with the whispering women or with the deceptive plans of Signor Barabo. Nor with the prefect's temporary arrangements for the captive, for he existed only for this, the torture that demanded no strength from his own arms, the turn of ratchets, and a blowing of bellows into live coals, his activity confined to the adjusting of his four hooks—a cunning that grew in the dark, that filled his lungs with the smut of burning hair and oil.

But I would sooner my boots pick up fresh dung by the hour, the rain splatter my bald skull, the ice stiffen my red cape, and the dwarf trees lash my shoulders at a run, than sit bent over, afraid to injure my windpipe, studying the silent drops of moisture on the aquiline nose of one being garroted in a cellar thick as a furnace. Signor Barabo could recite the canticles: "The hangman shall be four cubits tall or more, shall have a head of prominent bones and smooth on the top so that all admire the irrevocable round of the bone and largeness of brain, and he shall be bareheaded except on each day preceding the Sabbath named in advance by the hangman when he shall wear a pointed black cap the better to see him and to make the grimness of his nature apparent by contrast with the conical black peak, in the manner in which the fiercest animals are fashioned with some unnatural largeness of hindquarters, stripes on their sides, or horn."

Between the high tower and the low was a rampart of moss and stone, a catwalk connecting the two as stolid as a Roman battlemound. It led one at a level with the chimneys and unearthly shrubs. There was no hand rail, here the rock was soft and sloped toward the drop to the valley, narrow and red with the iron secreted in the crevices. I walked out upon this ledge, the wind swept it with his frost. As I moved, a large barren nest, insulated with old feathers, was suddenly flung into the air where it hovered a moment, a round tangle of black briar, and, striking an invisible pit, fell down heavy as a demon's iron halo.

The low tower barely held one man. I was able to look over its edge into the silence below. It was a mere turret fashioned from the silence of the fortress, protected from the wind, and covered with drops of moisture like the hollow of a tree trunk. To wait here and to watch, confined in the lookout overhanging the quiet court, made my crossed arms patient and the eyes dilate as through the gray of the dark. The stone that came to my chest hampered even the intake of breath, yet at that moment I might have already fallen, stepped into the beating air.

The tall lady stood below in the court almost as if she were taking the sun. Now she had no rope. Her place had been appointed by men who with trepidation paced off the earth and tasted it upon their knees under her shadow, a shadow taken to the earth and remaining there. The scaffold itself, shaped like a tool of castigation, was constructed to support the dead weight of an ox if we came to hang oxen. She was of wood and black as a black ark, calm by nature, conceived by old men with beards and velvet caps, simple and geometric as frescoes of the creation of the world. She offered no retraction or leniency once death was in motion. Much about Sasso Fetore was told in the idleness of the gallows. And idle, without her tongue, how stolid, permanent, and quick she was, still ready as the roots of ancient speech for the outcry. Her shadow changed sides while I watched and it became more cold. The sun did not come too close to her.

"Grace to you, grace to you, Hangman," shouted the citizens of Sasso Fetore and put flame to their torches though it was still light. The faces in the crowd that formed on the swept cobblestones when the prisoner was hurried into the fortress, the faces whose noses, cheeks, foreheads—of a greedy man, sullen man, obedient man, choleric serf—struggled to free themselves from the caricature putty and paint of their daily look. There was a murmur, the press of the people, in expectation.

If Signor Barabo had come upon me then, he would not have bothered with his long practiced and formal "Permetta che le presenti mia figlia" nor bothered to bow or hide the worn patch in his official cummerbund—he was flushed and might only have shaken his head at the obvious color and fulsomeness of his daughter's arm. But he remained now behind closed doors in the caffè and the glass before him was kept brimming.

"My eldest daughter—gentlemen, Antonina—has become the belle. Let us be bold: the word is *appassionato*. Already, sirs, I seek to hire two backs at least to carry the dowry, two more her gowns and the rest of it.

"Let us call her 'respected bride.' Donna, but we can agree, every bone in her body is true, the knuckles are hard and the heart does not flutter needlessly. Put your coats down, gentlemen, for my daughter.

"She has been standing these seven years—confident the while—in a pasture of chilly reeds and not once has the wind spied her ankles. Have you seen them, gentlemen, the virgins touching each other's cheeks by the mill or the lonely south crèche?

"But, gentlemen, even the little girls titter when my daughter passes. The children suspect something, my friends! Will it be the white gown or the gown the color of pearl? The embroidered linen or the plain? Shall we order radiant dignity? Will we serve pheasant and fish or goose? What sort of rings? I ask you. I ask you to think of Antonina...."

"There is Lucia, also, Signore."

"...Yes. And of Lucia also if I may ask it. Think, gentlemen, for your pleasure and make your decisions. The baking must begin at once. For I tell you, the weddings will sweep us like grass fires ...."

Signor Barabo rubbed his hands as if he were rolling a great ball of unleavened dough, the fathers of Sasso

Fetore raised the bowls to their lips in salute. A small lizard ran across the floor and the coffin maker reached out his boot and destroyed it against the beam. There were two narrow windows in the caffè, each filled with small thick cubes of purple glass sealed by lead into the frame, through which, thick, opaque, the street and the world beyond were dimmed.

And out in the street thronged the crowd. A few, grinning uncontrollably, rapped on the glass, an aimless communication of the drift of their mood. The emotion went among them, possessing their hands and feet, making them noisy. Those who had been asleep asked, "When did he come?" "Citizen, only one of them?" "When will we see him again?" Some, with uncomprehending eyes and jaws slack, shouted, "The hangman has taken his wife, he has taken his wife!" knowing not what they said.

They put their hands upon Antonina, crying, "Fortunate, fortunate, she here will not have her purse for long ...." The women dropped combs from their hair. Now two, now three, fell from the crowd and stood looking at each other with wonder. Signor Barabo's wellborn eldest daughter, Antonina, was no more able than they to resist the street crowds. She walked in the direction of the Jesuit's chapel, but she did not enter it. She was reluctant, yet Antonina, also, was not to be denied and climbed to the heights of Sasso Fetore, as women will when they have heard of a disemboweling or other fascination. She did not shudder seeing her sisters with the cloth off their shoulders.

Antonina was one of the virgins who have grown knowledgeable as an old wife, select at nursing fires or calling back the dead with circles and chalk. Up she came through the rose campions and sourweed, having refused the accompaniment of Little Ginevra, and the tears of the brisk wind were impersonal upon her cheeks still olive with the pigment of generations.

"Antonina, Antonina, this way," hailed Signor Barabo from the door of the caffè and waved the handkerchief he had lately shaken at the prisoner. His daughter gave him the rare crow's wing of her smile. "Gentlemen," shouted the father, "behold!" And they gathered behind him in the door frame, a dozen pairs of eyes and a dozen goblets.

In a curious manner, with intoxicated bravado and a fear lest the words not be said at all, Signor Barabo shouted his daughter's banns loudly, each time incomplete: "Antonina, respected and loved of father and mother, has become betrothed by law and by permission of her father, soul, spirit, and good temperament to Signore…" "Gather the white flowers, gather the white flowers, Antonina shall marry…" "It is declared, this woman's betrothal has been fixed on earth and I, the father, give her, I give her…" And these speeches— he was clutched by his compatriots in the doorway — were addressed to the oglers nearest him, the red noses and scar cheeks of the women who replied by opening their mouths as if hearing a proclamation of punishment instead of the banns. Then he freed himself and pushed a way toward his daughter. "Will of the Donna that she marry, will of the Donna that she enter the rooms of the tall booted hunter; no daughter shall refuse to give herself and her father asks it. All the public shall see her enter the stranger's house, none see her return. Begone to wedlock, then!"

He took her arm and stepped forward, bowing to the left and right, low, and the integument wriggled under the coat between his shoulders. Antonina was a head taller.

"Un momento, per favore," muttered the coffin maker, catching up with them and pulling after him his daughter Lucia. The two pairs climbed the black and white streets. Black rings and bolts, white stones once washed by the sanctimonious noviates, how the wind whistled in them, preparatory to thundering down the mountain. The two old men held tight their virgins. Antonina, despite disbelief and the black band fastened about her throat, walked sternly a little in front of her father, hastening to see for herself. Her face was like the Donna's. Already she knew what propriety was lost—but Antonina's heart made public would perhaps put them to silence. Her mother, deftly, had pinned a small male figure of silver to her hip and there it caught the sun.

The red and the gold was gone from the fortress. Signor Barabo took his daughter in Pucento's late footsteps, grimacing as the shrubs slipped through his hands and he tottered, wiping his face. The fortress was black and white with age, the rooks screamed the cry of a dying species.

Signor Barabo stared up at the grated window of the fortress and as soon as he got near, he bellowed: "My

son-in-law, future son-in-law, look here!" stamping his
foot and shaking his black hat in the evening, unconscious of the shadow at his side.

I, on the other hand, took my usual ride that evening.
Despite the disturbance among the people, the graveyard was still and softly grained as an etching. Since
some had worked this day, I passed the trees still smoldering, the stunted pines whose roots they labored to
destroy by burning. I rode across their farms and through
the middle of Signor Barabo's villa as well. There were
no signs of the young women waiting out upon the rocks.
Perhaps their mothers were plying them with mulled
wine. Certainly they were not teaching them any matter of weights and measures—even the women of Sasso
Fetore were acute in the practice of weighing sin in their
hands like a pound of oats—the sciences of law and balance being this twilight abandoned for the plaits of the
true lover's knot.

I did not stop. My donkey trotted jangling past the
very light from their windows, so close his hoofs shook
the earth of their floors, but there was not a question of
my dismounting, not a movement to detain me though
the donkey brushed the sides of their gates. One would
hardly know what they were thinking, except that I saw
a creature leaning over a hooded well and, through the
dark, laughed at her reflection in the green water. And
in front of a hut there fluttered a fresh veil on a tilting
weather-beaten post. The women of good station and
poor were distracted from the bedrails, the pitchers, the

pillows grown small and brittle under their heads. Large women such as Antonina now fitted their bodices in the moonlight.

The farther I rode from the city of Sasso Fetore, the better was the view of the fortress, large and silhouetted, black and irregular up there as the multi-prisoned bastile town of Granada. What fate had it to offer the husband hunters! Or the fathers also who, had they the stock, would have busily slaughtered the hogs and cut from them the delicacies of the viscera to be served black and steaming as roasted chestnuts.

To turn one's eye from the immediate rock, the cannibal briar crouched under cover of some phosphorescent leafy plant, from the immediate valley road crooked and hard to the rider, to twist about in the saddle and back there, high, far away, see the white fortress and its stripes and shadows, black with its secrets, terraces, barred apertures: the landmark forever there, from which formerly flew pennants of the "festa," now sporting crow's nests and rook's nests over the smell of dead lions in the arena.

The forest was full of activity; on all the trees the small twigs were newly broken and some trunks were still aglow with sparks. The donkey took me heavily through the underbrush, not starting at the fired tree trunks but shying testily when we neared the mouth of the cave. The tunnel, polluted during the time of the fairs, was now lit by torches, pitch sticks wedged deep in the rocks. They had picked the forest bare, dancing a quadrille almost extinct in Sasso Fetore.

The Donna stood before the cave, an idol whose nights were spent with a few small deer and speechless animals. The donkey turned a sharp foot, the lumbering saddle creaked, and even this far I saw the defamation, the Donna's face smeared with blood. I galloped. As I passed her I raised my boot and, ramming her chest, dislodged her so that she fell and rolled upon the crackle of the clearing. And there came the peculiar rush and windmilling, the sound of a bird striking in the dark the outermost protective net of leaves, as the owl first beat his wings attempting to penetrate to his roost at dusk.

The Synod and the Sentence

"Mi scusi, Hangman," cried the deputy, "it is time to assemble!"

The hunchback went first with his load of faggots and after him, one by one, the council entered, folding their way into the dark, the draft of the senatorial chamber. The old men took their places at the table and awaited the burning of the fire which was preceded by a cold unsuccessful time of acrid smoke. The hunchback kneeled and blew, twisting the faggots with a bare hand, poking his tongs.

"You too then, Hunchback, you have a daughter." Monco peered up and grinned at me, splintering a twig with his knife, and I at him, for Teresa was a girl who should have been burned in Sasso Fetore. He tore a bit of rotted cloth from his sleeve and fed it to the sparks; nothing burned so well for the firekeeper as what he wore. But it was a slow fire and there was whispering at the table.

"A man with a daughter, your honor—Grace to you for having none—cannot think of cutting wood!" grinned he again, lifting his lamed back like a tortoise.

There were twelve seated at the table, far apart and separated by such broad wood that now and then they put their bellies upon it, stretching the whispers. About their throats they had tied the traditional magisterial ruffs, collars like honeycombs of rag paper. The uncomfortable ruffs scratched as they talked, louder and louder with the hurry of the words. Each had a gavel fashioned of rolled calf's skin.

I took my place at the head under the tester blazoned with the escutcheon of a burst fess, a black leathern tapestry from which the dust was never blown, reputed to have once been the skirt of a barbarian conqueror. To conquer without going to field, this spirit of mettle was vested with predaciousness in the hangman.

"Grace to you, grace, grace," said each as I sat and the first deputy posted himself at the door, carrying athwart his broad sword. The fire sprang up and the hunchback and my ward—Pucento was weary and laughed the more—both on their knees pushed and knocked the live coals across the flagging.

"How does the prisoner sleep this first night, is he cared for?" asked Signor Barabo. Before the question was done, Pucento shouted, "Hooks!" and put his forehead down to the stone like a frothing jester. The reeds from the fasces were still bound about his thighs and ankles and some, catching a spark from the embers, smoked, shriveled to black char.

The judgment supper was served, a formality that appeased the instincts of the council, food thought to bind the officials to the hangman and to perpetuate the feast of the law body which preceded Sasso Fetore's original compulsory execution. Before each place was set a platter containing a fish, as long as a hand and thin, speckled green and served whole with the tail and head gray-black in color, bright and opal. I cut my portion with a three-tined fork and a dull knife, but it was customary for the councilmen to take the fish, and its slight dressing of oil, up in their fingers. The river diet was never changed, each day the hunchback wedged his sieve traps into the rocks of a vapid waterfall and awaited his catch, relishing most the moment when it was time to pile the ash together on a peeled stick, thrust the point through their blinking gills.

The thirteen waxen fish, lying straight on the porcelain platters, were devoured again; the councilmen once more broke the tough skin and immobile, formidable under their broad brims, separated the white from the myriad hair-sharp bones. The fish was bitter, its meat came apart with the elasticity of muscle instead of flakes. Occasionally there was a portion of small black roe. This was the cuisine of justice, by firelight the minute fish and the pointed fins were illumined, sticky, each one silver and half-picked against the great black of the benches and under the gray hands of the councilmen. The fish was the fare of all the verdicts delivered and with its complicity of bone and deathly metallic flesh, it had the character of a set jaw and seal ring. It was by the fish that the jurists earned their title Mongers. The season of salting the furrows with the fresh water's spawn was the season of many bells when the Mongers brooded upon those to die.

A food of no sweetness, small pleasure, but the same distributed at the council of Bishops and Gaolers, the same that stuck painfully in the throat of the past— Signor Barabo ate his share quickly enough. He was heard to mutter, "Bella, bella," between mouthfuls though the meal was declared a period for silence. He was tired of seeing each morning begin with the scrubbing of his daughters, was glad now his wife might put aside the wet bundle, her broom. Signor Barabo was volatile and held the fish up by its tail, the shadows taking dark hold of the ragged cavalier cut to his uniform.

I rapped my knife on the table and passed it twice sharply in front of my face, blade toward the lips. Signor Barabo, fat as he was, pugnacious as he was, kept himself quiet after that. The twelve old men concentrated until the last of the fish was gone. The hunchback went down the left side then the right, taking the plate from each as he was supposed— assuming the familiarity that might be expected from the serfs with their rock plows or from the wine pressers—tapped each councilman on the shoulder so that the citizen should be represented and their fraternal feelings, like the tipping of a hat or the offering of swine for mercy, should be expressed. But he did not touch the hangman. When he took my plate, setting down the tall stack of the rest, he pulled a crust from his pocket and rubbed it in the remnants of the fish oil. Then ate the crust.

The moon appeared beyond the high windows criss-crossed with iron. The moon, having suffered in the heavens some voracious attack by night-migratory flocks, its face having been picked by the wind, drifted low past us now in shreds of yellow against the darkness, and disseminated the cold of its center over the roof tops, the priory buildings of the fortress. Inside, the fire took some of the chill from the room. Yet it was cold with the damp smell of their boots, beards, brown hands, and with the machinations within the councilmen's heads, each one thinking his own daughter the kindest of tongue, the best of proportion, and the keenest to do marital bidding.

The old men were dressed alike. The men of Sasso Fetore, and the Mongers with them, at a distance could not be told one from the other except by shape or peculiarity of walk, and these marks too were not obvious when they were gathered in crowds. The brown shirt and the wide-brimmed black hat covered all of them. There was hardly a variation, earthen cloth for the back and a headgear adopted from the primitive monastic order whose members worked in strict obedience and were the first inhabitants of the province. So the shirts were still the brown color of the lay members' robes and the black hats unmistakably derived from those creatures who chanted while fighting on the early slopes of Sasso Fetore, pair by pair beating each other with hard fists under the watch of Superiors—these same fighters who during the matin scrubbed the garments of the sick and diseased on the rocks by the river where the councilmen's fish swam.

Despite Signor Barabo's sash, the twelve Mongers sat before me in such lowness and humility, the fattest and oldest for all their years and their daughters still covered only by the cloth brown as the furrows and dead grapes, the brown that flooded far as the black and white posts of the border. The hunchback's fire and the cold-smoked walls of the chamber allowed no other uniform for the tribunal: by common dress the disparity of their height and features should be shown trivial and in no way belying the meanness of men.

The first man to rise, rip open his hempen shirt, and expose his breast was allowed to speak, the rest thereafter not needing to perform this ritual. That night it was Signor Barabo who could not tear at the buttons quickly enough, scratching the white skin in his haste. The others, who remained seated, buried his first words with the crash of their gavels. Antonina's father revealed greater and greater portions of his chest, appealing to that which he was not and could not hope to be.

"Hangman. *Boia savio. I* asked if he was well cared for," he began. "There was no answer. I sought to learn if he slept and was not gratified. And I climbed to the fortress, *Boia.* Yes, straight up without admiring the view and risking myself to the steepest path. I called 'Son-in-law!' using that familiar term. His face was easily seen between the bars and brambles but even from him there was no answer. It is boding. What has been done to him already? Are we not to welcome him when the sun warms us?

"Look at me. I show my chest and part of the belly also, and I ask: *Boia savio*, what is to be done with him? Are the dead to be made jealous for nought? Who would make Antonina—think for a moment that she is not mine—who would make Antonina shudder again? Must our young women walk with their faces forward and forever scanning as if they be the figures with salty bosoms leading ships by iron noses into the gales? *Boia savio.* Not she.

"Should not my son-in-law walk freely? What have I but to take his fecundating germs like pieces of eight for my daughter? And to let him build some cradle, gentleman's cradle, if he can, out of the deep. I've thought of it, so I might lean myself between the two of them when my old wife is dead, and hang to the arm of each when they take me airing. I'd hurry my decrepitude for that. No one else, Hangman, has come or here offered himself as yet....

"And yet my knuckle, with the rest, has surely tapped their breastbones, and in the past we've hung them. Rather you have hung them, *Boia*. What will our justice be? If it is a white card—a white card, *Boia savio,* what mercy!— think how my son-in-law will sleep with his snoring and rise early to stretch his white legs, while I sleep late! Think how Antonina will lift her eyes! Who knows what his inheritance might be.

"I would have it so she will her husband, one to whip

the hostlers when the hostlers return, and be regenera-
tive after she has collected a thousand lire of his passion.

"That. Or hang him high by the law?

"Which?"

I gave him my answer. He shook once and attempted
to button his shirt. It was as if I had ordered his soul
bled from the arm, and Signor Barabo sat down. It was
impossible for the old man not to betray himself, his
disappointment physical and evident as the rings round
the owl's eyes. He looked at his fingers, thinking vaguely
there should have been large blood-gems set upon them.
I gave him my answer again, abjuring him, and the
Mongers listened on either side of him with faces like
millstones, turned to profile and blinking. There was the
coffin whose face was nailed together, the cart with his
elbows resting upon his wheels, the wealth of land and
his earth belly, and Signor Barabo who was not loath in
his heart to see the prisoner die. This oligarchy—the mud
of their thighs no better or surer to last than that of the
old man who left his rake to watch the prisoner pass—
was yet familiar enough with the ancient tongue to understand me, these old masters having in their histories
sentenced not a few.

High over our heads there was a rustling, a tearing as
of a sailsheet, and from a nest suspended by the beams
dropped a half-stripped bone to clatter upon the table.
Signor Barabo asked to excuse himself. Monco the
hunchback burned the last of the fish in a heap on his
tall fire. The air of longevity was strong, the Mongers sat
straight as those before them, it was a hall in which the

lizards in summer, the rats in winter, peered at the justice of Sasso Fetore captured in oil paint, the noses and downturned mouths preserved by the sculpting twist of the palette knife. The building had a flat roof and was surrounded with arcade and flagstaffs and marred by the slings of barbarians. It was the only white building in Sasso Fetore. Here, this night, we conducted our business despite the look on Signor Barabo's face and while he trod through his dreams keeping one hand on the pocket where he carried a curl of Antonina's hair.

How long shall be the length of rope? That was decided.

And the braid of the rope, fine or coarse? That was decided.

Was blood to be drawn first from the throat or not? That was decided.

And who shall be witness? Also decided.

At last Signor Barabo began to wake and to his brothers' voices added his own yea or nay. Still he interrupted to murmur, "The respected bride, the respected bride," and sharpen his eyes as if to contemplate the beneficence of this title, yet envisaging a wedding summons of four quaint pages.

The firelight seemed to come out of its hiding, their faces became white and more round. There was a cut to their lips and a leathern round to the knees beneath the table. The hunchback—the rock that bowed him rose on his spine higher than the head—waited upon each old man with an iron pot and from it doled half a hand of ash on the wood itself in front of each; to each he gave a quill and poured water over the ash, the writing fluid thick and black and staining the wood. They commenced to scratch and blot the document as it passed up and down their row.

"*Attenzione,*" they again would read along with the rest from the northern wall, "*Attenzione...*" I could see the rain beating the shoulders of those who depended upon nothing so much as the formality, stringency, the trueness of ring, the evidence of the Death Decree. "*Attenzione!*" Always the Decree contained the name of the condemned. It was the task of the citizenry on hands and knees to scrub the piazza after the execution.

"*Boio savio.* Antonina would wear twelve skirts to her wedding." And he wrote his full illegible name in the script that once flowered in this country. But Signor Barabo was also a cruel man, as his daughters told.

"My daughter, Altezza," grimaced the hunchback, "would wear none!"

My face showed nothing. Like long trained and impounded clerks, the old men dropped their quills and took up the gavels: "Grace. Grace to thee, Gufo." And they followed me into the night, leaving the faggot-gatherer to quiet his flames. The Mongers huddled together and waited to see me depart before dispersing, before touching each other's shoulders silently and descending alone to their several rooms, knocking secretly on the thick doors in narrow streets. Think of them then finding their way about among their personal belongings, correctly choosing the bed, the roughened walls, and those who have kept awake for them. How unsearchable is the law whose sentence they subscribe to and which leads each home and to a sleep that continues while the chimney cools! We left them, Pucento and I making a hard noise up the slope.

We went the way from the senatorial chamber to the square of the tall lady, past the hangman's leaning house and stable, and up the highest rampart broad enough to permit a cart of fifteen unfortunates to travel—before dawn and with hands roped—to the gallows. A few posts like black briar still remained driven into the rampart; from these Pucento hung out, peering, a bare-headed silhouette, toward the nightly star-spaced distance that drifted over the whole of the valley.

"Padrone," my ward pointed and whispered, "the prisoner."

Up there was a window and two thick bars, a window secreted in the crevices of the fortress, an opening eaten through the stone so small as to hide the features of the prisoner and stop his cries from passing to the air.

The portcullis was only an arm's length over the prefect's head. There he stood idly, a truncheon dangling from his wrist, and smoking a short butt of cigarette.

"Buona sera," he whispered and made a gesture to straighten the two straps snarled across his breast. "A respite, *Boia*," he said softly and shook the fingers of his truncheon hand as if they were stiff and pained him. He had oiled the keys and they glistened at his belt, those that opened the locks of coffins as well as the fortress door. He smoked and the thin substance of his cheeks stretched over the bones to the mouth. He shifted, the rotted pumps on his feet scratching the ice and gravel, and he glanced between the teeth of the portcullis toward the clouds.

"Will it storm, Hangman?"

"Prefect, I will see my prisoner."

Still he put no life into his marionette arms and legs, thin akimbo creature resting, inclining, bedraggled in his official position. Then he began to study his keys as if he did not know them well. Sullenly he thrust them toward me.

"Can you choose, Hangman?"

I chose the large bull-headed key. Yet he did not move. To the west stretched the topography of our lowlands— the snow was collected in the pits and gullies and with the flat white shape of salt encrustations gave tooth and rib to the night, dimly providing a body for the dark. The low possessions were there, wind-swept, across which barked Pucento's fox. The prefect's name would never be scratched on the floor of the senatorial chamber, nor would he have so much as a tombstone to slant abjectly through the lean centuries to come. He existed as at the mouth of the drainpipe to Sasso Fetore. But the prisoner was, for the moment, in his custody.

"I will need a lantern, Prefect."

"Carnefice. Eater-of-deer-horn. Will he not have a term of servitude? I should care for him, Hangman, as he deserves."

The prefect made this plaint and leaned more heavily, refastened the keys to the leathern girdle beneath his tunic. His kepi, with its battered top, was ill-fitting and crooked; it slipped far forward, giving outlandish shadow to the shape of his head. There was no sword in the scabbard which he still dutifully wore where most men in Sasso Fetore would carry a good hip.

"If he has not escaped, Prefetto, I will look at him."

The bolts fell. Pucento began a soft excited keening as we entered and, before we reached the dungeon, was calling ahead *prigioniero! prigioniero!* The prefect faltered with the lantern. I walked slowly, my footsteps paced. But Pucento ran suddenly, flung his body against the bars of the cell, and shouted loud as he could: "If we free you! If we free you, Mostro, will you not ask for the hand of Little Ginevra!" And Pucento panted, the straw on his wrists and ankles rushed against the wooden bars.

"Look now, Hangman," the prefect swung the light at arm's length, "and decide, per favore, to leave him with me."

For now the prefect was the proprietor, knowing only too well of the young girls who were ready to bribe unmercifully for a sight of his charge: malignant, with a show of pride he turned the best possible light upon the prisoner.

The floor was dirt. Through the high window I saw a cold star, then a few flecks of snow. The cell was short, the eastern wall a ledge, stony and down-sloping, upon which the prisoner was to sleep. A large wooden spoon and fork lay there and black thistles shedding pollen dust. At first the prisoner tried to protect his eyes from the lantern glare, then slowly he got to his feet.

"Mio prigioniero," I addressed him simply and said no more. He looked at me; and the prefect also, with Pucento, looked at me. In the recessed eyes was a worn pleasure and, in this fortress cell, expectancy. Here the prisoner was detained in Sasso Fetore's highest stronghold, a man with two hands, feet, and all the past we can remember, our captured image, a foreigner. He blinked less in the rusty light.

"Little Ginevra," muttered Pucento, kneeling, peering first at the prisoner, then at myself.

"Shall he take off his coat, Hangman, that you see him better?"

Every now and then the prefect shook the lantern as if to shake it into other focus. Nothing was the prisoner's but what was about him, little remaining yet all, the hair on his head, the gray of the skin around his mouth, the coat.

"No, Prefect. But unlock the cell."

"Donna. He is used to no one except me."

Pucento's round head, the round head of the prefect, the lantern's head were at my back in the doorway, and I faced him with nothing between us but the air which we did not turn to intelligible sound. He wore a gray trenchcoat that buried his legs; he was hatless, and on his face was an expression of wistfulness. His collar was damp as if he had been breathing quickly all his life, on the collar a silver insignia of a skull and crossed bones. The features, the teeth pressing against the lips, the eyes which had failed in his calculations now lay pale and aged with pupils in semi-focus. And yet all about him was the smell of earth, as if earth had been packed into his helmet, ferns packed in his sleeve, and the buttons, catches, and chevrons had rusted away.

I took his two arms and lifted. They remained outstretched, and I took hold of his lapels and pulled. I put my hands on his ribs and felt with care high as his armpits, slowly, and he remained standing despite evidences of the prefect's hooks. There was a lump on one rib as if it had mended of its own strength. He endured this inspection: and the while his attention, his form of halted intelligence, was upon me as if to find some information for his own welfare in a gesture of mine.

I was that close to him. And did not intend to be so near him again until the Pentecost was past. Still there was not a word from him, only the accumulation of strangeness, the signs that he would never be at home in the cell before we removed him. Never again quite locate himself, he who had lost his batallion of all things familiar and banal, his comrades. I suddenly found that it was with curiosity I searched him.

Under the coat, hanging from one shoulder, I discovered the black grained map case, much out of shape since he had slept on it, and across the front of the case were loops containing two thick writing instruments and a steel calipers. This I took and opened. A thin sheaf of maps was tied inside, a packet on thin paper and wrinkled with constant exposure to water. They were of our province, the details, landmarks of Sasso Fetore recorded precisely, the perimeter clearly indicated, the place of the charred foot soldiers, the forest, and there was the fortress. I looked closely. Then handed the case to the prefect. There was nothing else. Only that he had known his way to us by these directions, the work of an old and shrewd cartographer.

The cell was narrow, the ceiling low, and the earthen floor was covered with the many sharp prints of boots wide and thin, pointed or blunt. The red light honed the bars, and the two bars also in the window beyond reach. I wondered what ruse he might try to get his head up to the window, what efforts he had already made. He was perhaps sensible enough to catch a glimpse of the night and to remember his homeland. Beneath the natural height of the cranial cavity were the skull and bones and the enveloping wrap of the coat with its accumulation from long roads, and the great collar which had protected him from the winds when he followed behind the laborious gun carriage of his century. He was the embodiment of caution, the human form endeavoring for obedience and sustenance. I felt the beating of his heart and in that instant he too seemed aware of it and ashamed of it.

Had the women in the streets seen him at all? And Signor Barabo, paused in the caffè, sleepless, he too had overlooked the submission, the fated attitude of the prisoner who might yet be beaten to violence.

"Altezza." The prefect interrupted me and handed me a document that had been carried with the maps. It was written in the language of Sasso Fetore, faded and washed:

If I have fallen into your hands, treat me with human-

ity. While in your captivity, I should receive half pay in your own currency. No outmoded punishment should be practiced upon me in the name of the Spirit. The agreement is that I shall not be maltreated. You who take me abide by the charter. I am to have no fear for your charity. I will not give up hope. Regularly give me water and a ration. Honor, publish abroad a notification of my surrender that I may keep my place in the world, even in the separated ranks.

"Primo Boia," shrieked Pucento from his knees, making some sense of the paper, "tell him the truth! Tell him he will receive no visitors but these!" Pucento, my ward, reached up for the document, and I gave it him, with its notions of temperance and gothic print.

I stepped back suddenly from the prisoner and saw him sacrificing his last days to conversations with insects, growing a beard, and fasting without recognizing hunger. He would study his fingers closely, the expression of consequence would pass from his face until he was carried to the piazza of the tall lady. I saw a curious crudeness around his mouth. I looked at him, at the shape of his jaw, his height, standing with all the turmoil of his senses guarded, his knowledge serrated, and the skull and crossed bones were his last insignia.

I stepped away from him. That one human might inspect another, I peered at him and was aware of the declarations and betrothals within him. But, as he raised and bent his arms, I saw only the white tips of his elbows protruding from the sleeves in the coat. Signor Barabo's son-in-law! He was ragged! I would not remember him for long. Nor certainly would Antonina. I would not see him in such calm again. And then I shouted at him: "What is your name, *immediatemente!* Your name…"

He did not answer, and we left him in the darkness.

Pucento and I wound our way bottomward, both of us silhouetted at the rim of the cliff and against Sasso Fetore, its obstructing roofs and chimneys through which no one dared to call the watch of the night. The last lock closed behind us. It was late, the doors appearing in the darkness were not plumb. The nosegays of the welcoming crowd had been swept from the streets and they were deserted. The immense king's evil of history lay over the territory, and it waked me, as in the dawn, to breathe deeply, and I raised my hands at each doorway putting the seal upon them. Pucento careened ahead of me. Had it not been for the curfew, we would have been approached by those out of the dark begging their fortune. But the noose of night was drawn.

At my doorway, however—once we had passed under the arch and by the stilled Tuscan fountain—there was a disturbance, a fluttering and tangling with the bell chain, so loud that the old beast stamped in his stable. The prowler, come perhaps to intercede for the prisoner, was caught by the owl and, with fury and pointed ears, he sat upon her head, slowly raising and lowering his wings as a monk his cowl. He dug into her scalp, circumcising the brain. Her tresses were gathered against his dirty tail and he tugged as if he would carry her head up into the air. The owl labored and beat upon the woman, rasping through his gray hood. She tried to run, but he was fast to her and flapping, and the beat of his flooded wings slowed her.

I relieved her, taking the owl to my arm and comforting him. Pucento whimpered. "Little Ginevra," I said, "for your sake, you had best return now to your father." She fled and held her hair and the wounds in her wild youthful hands.

After a long while the owl's wings began to settle again to place, stiffly, with reluctance, the stimulation and traction, once summoned, loath to leave his wings and allow them to lie furled in sleep. They continued to preen and rise irritably as with the urge toward flight, ruffled, mobile, his mode of propulsion uncontrollable. But I wet and smoothed the feathers under the triangle of his beak with my tongue and he regained himself, once more folded into his nocturnal shape, and only the eyes did not relent. I gave him a large rat and slept near him the night.

And I dreamed of the universe of the tribunal. It was a closed sleep and a closed dream in which the tenacity of elements parted layer after layer to spaciousness. I dreamed of a brilliant morning and—I was remote, standing away—I saw the three turrets of the fortress rising each from its peak, and the mountain of Sasso Fetore off there was a pale green.

From each tower flew a small white standard, constant and square in the wind. It was a dream of the three white flags which were suitably the ensigns of Sasso Fetore, starkly bleached and deliberately unadorned with the hangman's owl. Their white was mounted briskly above the green. The country was no larger than the flags and as perfect. The road was a bright red line winding to the three precipices and the capital of rigid existence. And the flags were moving, fluttering, the motion of life anchored safely to one place.

A soundless wind. Then some silent battery commenced a cannonade from a distant point in the light of morning—not a figure appeared on the battlements—and a silent invisible grapeshot tore at the flags. The white standards were pierced and began a silent disintegration until they were no more than a few shreds beating solemnly against their masts in the blue sky.

And out of the blue sky came Monco's voice, wily and cold across the plains and fortresses, concealed in the rays of the sun: "The fish are running well. The fish are running well, Master," with mockery in his voice.

The Prisoner Escapes

"When shall we meet again, Hangman. When shall we meet again?" whispered Antonina, the belle, as if she would have the moment exactly.

Her body and her character were her contracts and she called me by name, Il Gufo. She had firm passions and firm words, and I felt the responsibility of her declaration made so clearly, and the question asked simply in the word of parting. *Appassionato!* She was white as the Donna these days and hourly grew taller as her love increased, and her passion was of moral seriousness to a woman who was herself a covenant. Even a woman such as she, descended from fourteen dames of wealth and modesty, might make her words sweet and sentient in her stand, the shape of her throat, the tone of her voice which was always of the clarity and deliberateness of the fire that could but burn so bright. Yet it consumed all there was. Absolute, dark-haired Antonina, her arms were thin, neither fairs nor family had trifled with her complexion. Under a green tree in a black field she read her sister the *Laws of the Young Women Not Yet Released to Marriage*—and in none of the laws was there heartbreak—while, her jaws moving, she cast inside herself the terrible beam of introspection. Hangman!

Quando potrò riverderla?

Little Ginevra was younger; Lucia and Teresa also were younger than she. They had not known the waiting. Their bridal purses were not as hard as hers, their heads not so high. Nor could they look upon the hangman and his equipment without shyness, and they aroused the owl. Antonina would have grown old loving the bleak rose campions and myself. She wrote no letters to the dead, but sometimes after I passed, she walked among them. One would have looked for her white gloves to reach around her darkest years, one would have thought to meet her at the green arbor. A stately, infatuated woman, she carried a love poison and a shawl for her neck and shoulders to the summer fair. At the fair she was met by Sasso Fetore's sisters, walking in pairs as if they had already ventured too far from home, coming from opposite directions bare-headed, unescorted.

Down the cliff they came, down the road like black angels, and I heard their whispering, the complaints of goose flesh on their arms. Hardly a woman or girl was left behind in the thin black streets of Sasso Fetore, vacated as they would be at the end of existence. But the field below was filled with the noise of feet that would kill the crabgrass, and I saw how few childbearers remained for all the pleasure they seemed to be taking and despite their demands for husbands.

From a clump of nearby bushes the old fathers of Sasso Fetore began to strum the viola da gamba.

It was now midday; the sun beat upon the field. Garlic was on their women's breaths, their appetites were sated with the macaroni that might make them milk. Little Ginevra was there too and wore the matron's wimple that covered her torn skull. They stumbled, the swaying shanks of hair, the flaming red scarves binding torso or hips and the cantilevering, the maneuvering of the skirts. Newly shod and gowned, the purple and green of earth and sky became warm in their presence; all that was female, unnatural in congregation, came into the open air walking as geese who know the penalty awaiting the thief who catches them.

Antonina had dark eyes. There was no girl's foolishness in her bosom. She was accompanied by her mother whose great square cheeks were white as salt. One dark and one white they passed, a tall one and a short, posting their two figures against the hagbush overlooking the field.

The fair was pitched directly below the fortress, in good view, and for the benefit of the prisoner up there. The black schism of the fortress fell thrice across our ladies' heads. In the silence of the hilltop, in the window, was the eye of he alone who could not join them. And I too, at that hour, felt the urge to climb again into the city. The owl and the prisoner remained and the women showed themselves freely, their voices drifted high and were suddenly clear.

History had forbade the fair, a guise for flirting and the dissatisfaction of a sex—the fair invoked only when the measures of fathers failed. I listened to the festival, the ribaldry of the viola da gamba, the concert of bushes. How could it be anything but an ill omen, the distraction and the gaiety of woman preceded the fall of man. Women could not be quiet when men met and stripped back the skin from their arms and presided over the bare bones of inheritance. What a time for the tithe of pleasure, as if the sun must assert itself before eclipse and radiate before bursting into the fens of winter.

For most of their days the women were threadbare, garbed for seclusion in gardens that were high-walled and bloomed only with a few sullen leaves. These faces were not classic, but in the charity of the fair one suddenly seemed good as the next, a dispensation granted to each with a large nose, eyes that were too large, and manners that were not proportioned. Like a useless cadre, the twelve Mongers stood in a line at the south limit of the fair, the brims of the twelve black hats touching and inseparably joined.

"If it pleases you, look at my daughter Lucia. Her mother has dressed her in brocade for the day." And there were more and more daughters; they promenaded on this slope where the lay brothers had fought with fists, and rope girdles entangled like fighting bucks, so long before the season when the field became spread with green.

"Mamma, I will carry your train. Un momento," spoke the very young, having forgotten the goats in the stable. The proclamation was wet upon the north wall. They had gold rings in their ears and other luxuries hung to their bodies. At just this fair in the past some were got with fornication and games, in the time when there were men to hang and those to spare, with clemency for neither.

"Attento, attento!" started the amusement and in the almond color of noon Pucento the lictor came upon the field. The women quieted and did not crowd beyond the small white markers but watched each beside her neighbor.

"To the hind legs!" Pucento shouted and proceeded slowly toward the center of the green. His walk was stiff, slow, itself determined by the beauty of the aged provincial combat between man and dog, the mastery of training over the temptation and distraction that plagued the low species. The women peered from the four sides, some scowling, some thrusting forward their cheeks withered as nuts, some smiling as if they alone were devoting themselves to a glassy pleasure at the sight of my ward high stepping and lean. The young girls watched covetously.

"They suspect something," murmured Signor Barabo and held Antonina by the waist, confidently. And where he stood also stood eleven Mongers more, their wind-troubled sombreros cut at different angles from amidst bodices, old women and their daughters.

The tempo of the viola da gamba increased, but there

came only the soundless winging of the musicians' bows, the silent press of the female hundred, and the stilled orderly panorama of the fair. The olive faces, the roses, the chameleon breasts were ranked and slightly moving under the hemispherical silence of Sasso Fetore. The noon tilted overhead. Antonina seemed not to feel the binding of the arm about her waist and did not watch Pucento for long but looked directly away and to the east, steadily. "Adesso," came the movement, the will of her lips.

When the dog turned, they turned, and the oldest and most grudging, with lace upon the brown of their chests, paid attention and swung the great fans atop their skulls windward, frowning through malignant black eyes as if they would not be fooled.

The streaks of the gowns against the earth, the moving flecks of the man and dog, the liveliness of the noon and the windy pasture below him were the last that he in the fortress would see of mankind, womankind. Each minute the grade up to the fortress became more steep and the music only a toneless drift from the strings soon to die.

The dog was muzzled. To the tip of the muzzle into a ring fastened at the end of the snout was hooked the leash which Pucento and the animal kept taut between them, a thin rein of brilliant red. Pucento held his arm, the fist gripping the cord, straight as long as he and the dog maneuvered together and the one obeyed the other. Pressure about the head controlled the animal; two leather cups on the muzzle hid his eyes.

On their leaning instruments the musicians played the seldom heard "March of the White Dog." This whole breed had once been deprived and whipped, tied ascetically by the lay brothers on the slopes. The bitches were destroyed. And the rest, heavy of organ and never altered with the knife, day after day were beaten during the brothers' prayers, commanded to be pure unmercifully. The dogs tasted of blood given in mean measure but were not permitted the lather, the howl, the reckless male-letting of their species. Beaten across the quarters, they were taught by the monks the blind, perfectly executed gavotte.

The sole remaining dog moved and balanced as the first packs, flawless, the long wail of refusal still in his throat and still denied him by the muzzle. The dog followed Pucento on the end of the tight rein, a heavy animal, the white coat become tarnished and cream with age. The women could not see how Pucento sweat, himself straining to duplicate the measure, the ruthless footstep of the past. Welts were knotted across the dog's hide, causing the hind muscles to be tough as if the leg's tendons themselves had been drawn upward and bound across the spine. The joints were round, distended, polished to silver, thick though the legs were slim, worn and delicate with the hours of balancing. But the meat, the shoulders and loins—tempered by the monks—were broad and considerable so that the animal might endure the requirements and travel long distances without touching the front paws to earth.

The old dog did not once attempt to snap through

the muzzle. It changed the rhythm of its gait perfectly and moved sideways with ease, crossing one set of claws over the other. All the desire, the reflex to kill, was still there under the white coat, inside the white skull and embedded the length of the spinal column, but Pucento had no need of the thick cane, no need to thrash the animal in the formality, the difficulty of the devilish dog's fandango.

First the two completed a square, then a circle, then the dog twisted and arched its back. Drawing down the quarters, it puffed and deflated its chest in one place, the leash pulling always the primitive long jaws and the restrained skull horizontally forward uncomfortably from the neck. But in this position the animal's silhouette was best.

"Attento, attento," they murmured again after silence and Pucento stiffened his arms, man and dog frozen on the green. Pucento spoke. The dog shuddered and swung backward in brutal symmetry, lifted, stood on two legs, then leapt, once, thrice, and each time a single leg only touched the earth, quivering, burdened, unnatural. On the one leg, the dog propelled itself upward again without falling, and the bones pressed through the fat. Even Antonina's mother did not regret the sight.

The dog stopped. As bidden, its front paws came to rest lightly upon Pucento's back on each side of the neck. Thus they remained rigidly, heads damp, white, lifted into the sun, while the musicians dragged their viols onto the field and the girls raised and silently shook their clutches of rose campions.

"Antonina," said Signor Barabo, "take your sister's hand."

But Antonina was gone and his arm was hooked only about his old wife's hip.

We climbed rapidly, Antonina and I, clinging to the steepest ascent. We pressed ourselves into the declivities of the cliff. The undergrowth, as it scraped the hand, was warm, now and then we moved upward through the devil's mace and were stung by the lonely nettles. Antonina took the path first and did not pause. She seemed to climb with her narrow shoulders, and there was spare straight movement under the twelve skirts. The music from the fair still reached us persistently up the bed of a mountain brook, La, la, la, la, so that we hurried. The women below trod across the green, a few disappearing off the edge of the slope.

Who has not wanted to climb on a warm day, up again toward the bare hills? We passed without thinking of the trickle of dispassionate water from the fortress. The air was clear and almost free of Sasso Festore's garnishing odor of rust and yellowed tomatoes. I drew closer to my companion. Antonina made herself known, and we climbed again.

The whiteness of the underskirts lay against the rock and coils of mountain grass. I heard my own boot slip and start, and I was behind her lest she fall. Antonina's pale hands touched the calcium encrustations of the rooks, and the wind took her face and clothes as if she had mounted those leaning steps to which the faithful will not return. Perhaps in her heart was good conscience for all her years.

Only that morning, so soon, she had distributed the contents of her bridal casks along the embankment to sun. After sunning them, she had made several bundles, tied them with cord, and carried them up the wooden ladder to the dark space beneath the roof, knowing they would not last there and that she would not need to take them down again. Her father would not speak for her.

And yet the thorn pulled at the leg, a trailing of her shawl was snagged in that steep place below the fortress. She swayed and proceeded to climb as if there would be more trysting. We were hidden by the glare reflected from the cliff, high where not even sheep grazed. In her hurry, her determination, she moved as if to absorb her indiscretion into the blood of her good family. Now she laughed.

At last we reached the ledge and stood side by side, then face to face so that I could not mistake her, Antonina. Not from weariness she leaned against the lowest walling of the fortress morticed agedly into the cliff. Already her breast was rising and the noon fled. We had no need to whisper, not even the birds were within rock's throw. But the wind was in our faces and we were temporary, though Antonina did not look as if her heart were sinking. The world this high creaked around us and, standing with no sure footing between the day before and the day after, she touched her bosom done with lightheartedness, spoke to me in the wind's way:

"Honorable Hangman. Carino. Il Gufo. It is you I love. I know what women do, and I have no fear of it. I have heard my father. I will be no belated bride. 'Not him,' they say. But it is you I love. I have seen you ride your jangling ass toward the rope readied and hung down from the sky like thunder. I remember the superstitions; I am old enough to remember them and you. 'Not him,' they say. But it is you."

And Antonina held to the leathern flanges on my hip, there on the cliff, among reed and empty eggshell. The fair was done; the waiting of rags done. I put my hand on her bosom and my hand met the two small silver hearts of a fine lady.

Antonina rolled stiff on the brown hilltop and the skirts loosened, lifted by the wind. She pushed her fingers into the bent grass and dragged her hair on the silt and stones. Her slender belly thrashed like all cloistered civilization among weed, root, in the wild of the crow's nest. I reached into the sheltered thighs touching this bone and that and felt for what all women carried. High and close to her person, secreted, I found Antonina's purse which she had hid there longer than seven years, that which they fastened to the girls when young. What was there more?

There was the prisoner. Having found his way from the room of four hooks, through the base passages, he climbed until he could go no further, bent and blinded by the light, clamoring into the air and to the stone above us scaled by no ladder or foothold. Now he freely cried *Guai!* Lifting his roving eyes away to the roofs, the spaces through the city, he seemed to fill his eyes with the distance to the borders. His was the rage of prisoners who climb quick as they can to the rooftops, who are caught in the tall trees—there was hardly that to steady him or give balance—reaching at last this windy free space. Perhaps the fair, the sudden quiet, the loneliness, made him understand that he could not escape the way he came. He was transmuted and prepared for the dizziness of the high ledge; the sun, the air currents, caught his face. I looked up at him and raised my hand to hold him.

The prisoner was covered with great feathers, pin feathers and flat feathers, pieces of wire and tin swelled his chest. The wings hung far down as arms and even below the hands, swaying, and were fastened across his shoulders. He crouched heavily, but his waxen feathers, his flying skein billowed angrily in the wind. His head stuck over with red wax turned loftily. Then he tested the wings, looking at the sun unbelieving, taking a cautious step closer the edge. The wings hung down and buried the arms inside; almost to the length of his feet, the tips waved like the lengthy, extra feelers of the dragonfly. The ends of the wings were wet, they motioned under the power of the primary feathers, the crudely fashioned wing with its sharp trailing edge. And when he filled the wings, they moved, lifted once, again, curving down and menacing. His half hidden chin jutted and thrust with the effort. He spread his legs and drew tight the red flying surface between them, so that he was a mass of machine and bird for the wind's picking. He appeared heavy as stone.

The wings caught, and he burdened the wings, the wax, and the red cowl from the rusty forehead. The skull and crossed bones were buried under the brown breast. He sapped the wings and his shod heels lifted, the knees flexing and ready to hurl him off. The eyes grew small in that headgear, birdlike, as if free they could distinguish only black and white and the long distance, in any direction, that there was to fly. None before him had thought of it, none fabricated such a means of escape. And his head raised, the urge to leave the earth and gallows, the very hilltop of Sasso Fetore, lightened the drag of the feet.

He tore himself away. He poised himself on the great stone and tried himself, peering aloft and away for some landmark by which he could travel and survive. The face was criss-crossed with red lines, he had discovered even the crop of the bird. The tail—for he would guide himself—spread out. Still clinging to the stone he wheeled once, then back again and pulled the feathers, not hesitating, merely tightening the tufts in the wings and drinking at the air. Behind him I saw the top of the low tower and the blue atmosphere. The wind blew up stronger and clear.

The wings beat slowly down. Then as if to break the bones in his arms, they were horizontal, sweeping a little windward. He brought his knees into the pit of his stomach and climbed toward open sky. The prisoner hovered, turned awkwardly, swooped close over our heads—

he kicked the air as he dove!—and sailed in a long arc up again, around, about to disappear across the witch's huts and chimneys of Sasso Fetore now darkening with the night already close. I saw him lastly fly defiantly through the smoke of Monco's deserted fire and into the red sun that sank and drew him down over the edge of the earth.

He Hangs

Finally the night enforced quiet. The tunneling cicada, the cicada taking the moonlight on patches of snow, were still. The shadows maneuvered, the eternal flanking movements and frozen sorties of the night were taking place. The brook ran cold and the mountain slopes, so far and of silver marched upon the rain, absorbed the moonlight like black cloth the sun; houses were deserted at dark when the fourlegged animals, not many, hung their heads. The fortress imprisoned only the empty hooks. The ice span told no time. There was the webbed fern, the rafter, the proclamation's promise, and the iron doors ajar—the bishops and gaolers done convening and taken to bed until morn. The galax opened its sharp leaves to prick the prowler, and there was an odor of night's roots.

The owl was awake, he swelled his chest, breathed

restlessly, and made himself known in the dark as if it were not deep enough. He was dissatisfied with the still lingering light and kept to his corner. Now and then, slow and purposeful, he eased himself from the pitch and moved in front of the window, his claws biting the ledge, his outline contesting heaven and plain, tree and pillar. He looked and the bare window was driven behind him, or blinked and was awake, frowning at the fortress and murmuring skies beyond the cliff. He looked so violently he heard nothing. Insects darted in and out of his feathers and they were nothing to him, so long did he stare to see that all was in the night as before, and before that. He looked steadfastly at the universe, then turned his back and proceeded to chew, pick, beat his cold heart, rustle so imperceptibly active with continuous life. Revengeful was he toward that which made him turn his white face and look into the dark.

He was old, scabrous at the window, he regarded the night from his stone and branch and all the night was preoccupied with some stretching of tissue or memory deep within the feathers, while rectifying the vision of the world in his owlish eyes, watching it as he might something that dared not move. He silhouetted himself and from that glance the night could not shrink into hiding in the atmosphere. He gripped Antonina's purse in his claw and now and then shook it, already it was ripped and musty as if it had been his forever. At times it fell to the window ledge and he kept near it.

Back and forth he went, continuously at work, conniving and busy with his feathers or lice eggs, watching the dark, flitching, flickering. He cut his bill on the stone, preened disinterestedly. Once, with slow effort, with a great plying of nerves and muscle he slowly shut his eyes, down, down, and obliterated the shadows, the space, and it ceased. Then, look, the dilation and they were round again, greater, the horned moons. He moved across the rim of his nest, Sasso Fetore, at the window. He outlined himself again and, face into the night, his head began turning so little, but sharply, right, left, and this was his alertness, something of all he saw aroused this speculation, something fallen upon that eye stirred him.

The owl carried Antonina's purse to the window and shook it. And the leaves in the scrub tree shook also. One claw was missing, another cut off blunt and short, at every feathered layer he was scarred and covered with old wounds that penetrated him like the grain of wood, his fiber, the old markings of the forest. But he had never cried with the pain, the scarred face, the face enraged and bloody, always anesthetized with the cold enormity of the eyes, the sudden circumference of the eyelids protecting him, making him insensitive.

Light began again to rise steaming from the earth, and from the owl's eye, slowly, lighted the knowledge of the day to come. He stiffened, watching the cicada stop, and all about his motionless body the hoary piercing feathers rustled in the breeze as if they were no part of him. He glanced at the frosted shadows, the warped tree laden with a winter provision of dead mice, at the cold pump. It was morning, but only he could see through the blackness yet heavy to the light that was kindling.

And he hooted, warning that someone was approaching up the winding road.

Signor Barabo came from the mist and halted near the window. He was wet, having come at this odd moment to take the owl's attention.

"Il Gufo. Boia?" He whispered, stooping and white. He looked up and bowed his head. He on the ledge waited. Signor Barabo stooped under his burden.

"I had not expected, Master…" turning his mouth on its side, whispering, squinting out of the frost. "For her I could not have asked you. Boia…Barabo's good fortune, I would not have missed it. Principale, I would reach up to you …."

On his back he carried a black trunk, rounded and banded at the ends. Wet black hair fell from under his broad hat, the face of whiteness and dark lines hung there, smiling, the neck bulged with labor. He had walked all the night.

"You must pardon me, Altezza," grunting, wryly twisting under the load, "two men could not be found. So I have come alone. Half the treasure is here, Boia." Once he raised his voice, "Dowry," he exclaimed. He stood at the edge of the cliff and his fingers clamped the brass handles. The black lines of the face, sweat-strewn, slyly peered upward. He had discarded the cummerbund and his ankles were thick with mud. "It is a pleasure, Boia, for me to bring this heavy load myself." Since sundown he had carried it.

And suddenly he dropped one shoulder, swayed as if he could bear it no longer, and the cask was loose, fell out of sight and split wide on the first rocks, smashing, and its collection of coins showered down the slope until all was quiet again.

"Ah, sfortunato!" His eye cut narrowly and he wiped his nose. Signor Barabo turned on a heel and, his voice coming as through the rain-drenched forest, "Hangman. Follow me." A gust of wind carried his hat also down the cliff, and with that, again he fixed upon the owl his nightworn face.

Pucento saddled the donkey. We set off in single file down the morning rim of the quarry of Sasso Fetore. Pucento walked at the donkey's head, limping, pulled the damp halter. All about was the stillness that follows fugitive action, and we proceeded through that time of dawn when the werewolf gives up his feasting and the assassin lifts his hands from the jugular vein of history. We met the first citizen in a doorway awaiting our approach.

"Triumph to your day, Hangman," and the citizen fell in line behind us until we met the next, shivering, and more after that, sentinels suddenly coming alive from the low entrance to the caffè and along the downwinding route, those who with their hands and feet, their persons, making no noise, pointed the path that we should take.

"Is it the same?"

"It is, Signor Barabo."

"They have not wakened perhaps in my absence?"

"They have not wakened, Signore."

So Signor Barabo questioned each. These men, as

they swung one after the other from niches and cold casements, out of the walls, followed us scenting and long-legged and sleepless, wet with uncomprehending vigilance. Over their brown shirts they wore short black jackets strapped high to their white throats.

"Power this day, Il Gufo," they murmured, surprised that I had come, and were gladly relieved.

The donkey braced his feet on the stones. It was not yet morning, the bells marked time coldly. No one peered from the windows, none proffered fowl or wine as we passed in single file. A gargoyle hid its face in corroded hands. I marched down through the people's hutch, thatch, sleep.

"Who lives here?"

"An old woman, Boia. She is asleep."

Even I had not seen this yard before. Under the hollow tile was an iron wall disappearing without vine or air hole into the earth. Leathern feet crowded and stirred upon her property while she slept, and the gate to her yard was open, pulled from its wooden hams. One had mounted the stones avalanched between wall and privy, silent, motionless over the others' heads, he watched the approach from the hill below. Another with large stride paced off the width of the yard and tapped his head grimly to remember it. There was tarpaper over the old woman's window, a trough filled only with a bed of fermenting straw, and the back step where she took the sun, all become cold and removed, visited by the dawn Mongers and the inquisitive strangers, because of the event perpetrated on this spot.

The deputation filled her yard like black chessmen thrust into the dampness and sands of ruin. The bony ponchos and black hats hovered to and fro, staring at the corpses in the idle chill.

The prefect was on his knees. His eyes protruded, the kepi was at his side. Signor Barabo sat down near the prefect on the trough of stinking straw. Traces of light began to flow onto the horizon with the roar of wind.

"Can you tell when it occurred?"

"Perhaps, Signore. Perhaps they have been here a few hours. Or more."

"And they are dead then?"

"Dead. They are cold, Signore."

The prefect's four ganders lay at the base of the iron wall and their white bodies were frost covered and gripped in the weeds, to be seen at the prefect's knees with all their dismal inertness and roundness of breast sparkling and portentous. They appeared white through the feathers, through the flesh, and to the earth. Their eyes lay like black berries half in the sand; through the bills the nostrils were bored with blue augers as worn holes in wood.

"Four hours at least, Signore."

The long-lying feathers were immaculate, though the wing of one bird was crumpled—fanning, uncomfortably jointed—against the black wall and hung there hazardous and spread as if it would defy the upsweep of air, no longer temperate, in Sasso Fetore. Otherwise, in the small space, they geometrically marked the four points of the compass, unruffled, exact creatures as they were left after death. The prefect did not touch them, he merely leaned further forward, put his hands upon the dirt near their circle and bowed so that the smoke from his cigarette burned his lip. He peered at the ganders who would no longer invade the impossible cliff top and campanile of Sasso Fetore, bedded down now emphatically in the place they would not have chosen to protect themselves from storm.

Not turning, with the smoke still branching and forking back from his lowered face, the prefect whispered: "Do you see the murderer?"

The one on the rocks hesitated. He opened his eyes wider, examined quickly the architectural slope and the ferns, and shook his head.

Signor Barabo's mouth fell as if to exclaim, but he remained silent. And one after the other the black figures rotated, stood a moment at the prefect's shoulder to look.

The ganders would no longer march through the steep places of Sasso Fetore, circling upon ridges, gables, spiked walls. No longer would they search the flagons— search the tall lady's piazza, the fortress, the field of dead foot soldiers—for the chaff and kernel of Flemish seeds, for a crack in the ice, for the remnants of dark days.

"They are dead, Signore, I feel it here. These are the lumps in the neck, there is a hardness under the bill, Signore."

And the prefect withdrew his hand, spitting away the smoke and tobacco.

The ganders had been felled carefully, symmetrical

and clean. The long necks, straight, each perpendicular to the next, were crossed one over the other near the heads, the necks touching and torn, left in their severed lines and with their cold windpipes in this intimate, unnatural pattern. The ganders, whose eyes gleamed logically, whose march was rhetorical, surmounted the prisoner's sudden inspiration to kill them and survived his warped and cunning urge to lay their bodies in crudely artful fashion.

The donkey rang his bells dumbly and none heard. The straw fermented. The guard on the rockpile lost his eyes into the mist and gave no alarm. There was no sign of the one who fled. Pucento, with tentative finger, felt over and over again the slashes imprinted on the earth by wingtips and fierce talons. Another stood waiting, and, from the wooden saddle, my feet slanting as iron and one fist upon the tin tattooed horn, I motioned them away, signaling that they leave their posts and wet odor of the yard. I pulled on the rein sharply.

The dawn became the color of the pear's belly. And not long from that time the prisoner's discarded, tall, half-broken wings were found abandoned against the whitewashed sidings of a stall. The straps that had bound them to him hung stiffly. In the mud his footprint was recognized where he struggled free. Before the Sabbath labors began, the citizens of Sasso Fetore saw for themselves the old woman's yard and filed past to stare at the wings by the barn where they were rumored to be. When darkness came again, the wings were illuminated with the flare of two torches and were visited even then. The children looked for signs of his toes in the wet sand, they whispered upon hearing the bell that was struck hourly as long as he was free.

And he was not free for long but was returned to the cell from which he had escaped, to the four hooks and put upon them. No one gathered at the fortress, satisfied with the announcement that he was there. His wings were splashed with kerosene and burned where they stood. In a matter of hours his cries commenced again, and peaceful anticipation possessed the owl. The citizens listened quietly as they stared at the pool in the grass, now empty. And the sun set. The crowd dispersed from the smoking wings that cowered, withered, fell to ash. Some days later—the prisoner was still suspended on the hooks—the skin was drawn away from his belly in one piece and stretched across a drum that was beaten through the streets while they stopped work and listened.

The Pentecost was past. The prefect, as was prescribed at this time, fasted and shaved his head. He was ready, imprisoning himself with the condemned until he should be brought to me. All of Sasso Fetore returned to read the proclamation with more care. The drumming upon the prisoner's flesh continued, sometimes the drummer was followed by women and the Mongers, sometimes he beat alone through the steady rain, and he took the old courses of the ganders, going nowhere in particular but marching and tapping the drum so that all would hear during the day. Sometimes the cries stopped and that too was heard. The old men waited in the caffè and they no longer spoke of Lucia or Teresa.

"Listen, Signor Barabo. It is past."

"Yes. And listen, thou, do you hear him hammering?"

"Yes. He is coaxing his noose and knot."

"Il Gufo."

The owl waited for the drummer to come, and each time bestirred himself so that he might watch. He sanctioned the herald to stop and to strike four extra beats for the owl and move on.

The millet grew ripe and hampers of blood apples were left in the hangman's piazza. A stone of bread was left also. Those in the caffè waited and made no move to kill the lizards that came from their caves in the fireplace; the bent grass sprang up again near the wall in the old woman's yard; the rooks flattened themselves in their nests on the cliff. The fox came into the streets but was not noticed, traveled up and down my road. Pucento brushed the donkey's black trappings, the monarchial owl stared about the proximity of the execution. The prefect buried the ganders, and Sasso Fetore had nothing else to think of, nothing else to prepare for.

One morning the drumming ceased. The fox hastened back to his hole. The bells ceased. Monco did not fish that day, and the fish remained deep in their pools. The cicadas were hushed. The cries were hushed in the fortress, the prefect giving the prisoner water from a tin cup. That morning Signor Barabo saw nothing of his wife and daughters. The fortress towered its three parts over the city and nothing stirred.

The yellow hammers appeared and flew into the sun; and the rose campions speckled the hillock, the path by

the headstones. Sasso Fetore was raw with the sun that
fell headlong upon the unoccupied streets and before
the campanile, the waiting city. Bright, clear, reddening
the cliff, the sun rose and spread down across the
unlabored fields. There was silence. None came from
their shelters while the shot of the sun tore at the white
flags raised on the bare masts and shone upon the as-
cending slopes with their briar, a few huts, inviting the
spirits to come again to that empty plain. All day the
sun warmed the copper in the eyes of doors and dried
the tall lady in the piazza.

"Listen," murmured Signor Barabo, "it has stopped."
And they listened, not venturing from the dark. It was
a day during which the citizens sat until they must
change a knee or arm and whispered while the sun
swelled the streets with the light. No meals were prepared, but now and then they drank small quantities of
spumante or Rosolio. They had not forgotten the long,
white, and crossing necks, nor perhaps their daughters.
They had not dared to right the Donna. The Mongers
themselves could not escape the superstitions, even when
the sun whetted the gardens and filtered to gleam upon
the wine presses.

The crabgrass grew again. The old men did not attempt to seek their neighbors; those who were already
congregated when this day came remained so, waxen
within the cellars or the caffè. No one gave thought to
attiring the young women in hammered silver and lace.
The council of crisis and the occasion of tragedy reached
them during daylight hours and when the sun was high,

Sasso Fetore was lighted the whole day and filled with the ferment of the sun rays. The day passed.

Only at dusk did a soft murmuring, the dialect and talk, start from the houses. Then some tried to remember the prisoner's face and they haggled over who had touched him and who not. The old woman who had proffered him the roasted fowl declaimed that she had retrieved it whole again, that he had not a chance to bite into it. The fathers would not speak a word to their daughters.

When it was dark Pucento carried in the kegs of grain, the bowl of blood apples, the pail of dissected chicken, the spice and paste and fish packed in leaves from the piazza. He built a fire using the tinder and flint intended for the Donna meat and the strips of white fish on the stones and the fat drained into the fire, crackling and hissing. He brushed the earth from the blood apples and steamed them until they were soft and strong of odor. He cooked black twigs that tasted as chicory, and the water boiled in the pan, the bones fell from the fish, the skin and meat became tender and dropped loose. Now and then he returned to the court and discovered another homage food deposited there, perhaps a vegetable the color of rattan. And this he cooked. He found a bucket of eggs no larger than walnuts. He boiled them. And he replaced the eyes in the fish heads. He stirred, snipped, built up the fire, and we drank cognac. One small bird he roasted and this he stuffed—showing his teeth and pushing his thumbs—with a handful of green grass pale and fresh. He burned his arms and did not notice, he worked his knife on the block and he bled; the blood apples broke their skins and he took them from the rumbling water with his burned fingers.

How different from the Mongers' fragile fish or the square dark loaf and water! The pewter was filled, the flat leathern platters smooth as wood were filled, and the chicken stones, the sticks wet with fat, the hearts like cherries and the joints, the twists of bread, were devoured, heaped up and then eaten. The owl sat long with a large and savory chunk of white meat in his bill. The smoke backed into the grate and was filled with the moisture of feasting. Pucento scooped at the black fish roe; I ate the sickle-shaped sections of a fruit and the fire lighted our red hands. Pucento sat with his elbows between his knees, his cheeks wet and his eyes heavy. Until the meal was done and the intestines could not move.

The donkey's freshly polished harness hung on the wall; the casket containing the rope was ready.

"I shall see Little Ginevra, Gufo."

Yes, and the rest of them. And the meal, torn from the anatomy of conscience, sat upon us, from the quantity found and cooked so seldom there came the effulgent memory of execution, step by step, dismal, endless, powerful as a beam that transudes our indulgence on the earth, in Sasso Fetore. There was suddenly the morrow, the way the brain sees death suddenly, and there was the penalty that could not be stayed. Lastly we chewed mint leaves.

In sleep there were the fantastic shapes of the food,

the sensation of looking forward, searching ahead into the rubrics burning upon the slopes of the rose campions. Gathered about my bed were the hangman's articles. The gloved creatures of dreams paraded all night and a hundred times I settled the noose before dawn, and straightened it and turned it.

And the eye opened to find it cold, partially light, silent; the windows were open, all pushed a crack or flung wide, and the door was off its latch; the cold had come early and lay about the rooms. I rose, strapped a wide belt around my flesh. The stones were cold. I saw the ledge, empty and small, wet, from which the prisoner jumped. Pucento slept in his clothes and the lips were pulled back from the teeth. I shook him and he waked, clutching at my chest, and said: "Is it over, Il Gufo, is it finished? Have you hung him without me?" Then leapt from the bed and brought my cap and cape.

The crowds were in the piazza before us, ranked on four sides of the tall lady and pressing close to the gallows of white hickory. The empty arms, the cold hands, were folded and skull touched skull. I climbed to the top, the platform, and Pucento crept to the bottom, into the small space where the prisoner would fall. My footsteps crashed above Pucento's head and down there, out of sight, he crouched back against the wood and hid his face, trembling, sick as upon sea water, cowering in the darkness lest he be struck by the descending feet.

I stood. I might only have been searching the countryside from the low tower or kicking a splinter of glass down to the rooks. I looked over their heads through the slits. The soft black horn atop my hood curved forward and shook slightly in the wind. And the red cape, the collar of red, was short and left my arms free. The gallows faced the fortress. Not an old man, woman, and child but what was here and stooping in his brown shirt, gray cloth, and thinking of the book from which their hangman knew the terms and directions, the means and methods to destroy a man.

The wind blew and there was the odor of the hemlock at the border. The bare firmament of the cliff was hidden behind the heatless crumble of Sasso Fetore. The cold and dripping hole waited in the tall tree. My ward, of all of them, was sick under me. With my fists I tore the eyeslits so that I might see further and see them from such dilated eyes. I passed, shaking the horned hood at them and stopped.

The prefect brought the prisoner quickly from the fortress, under the portcullis, down the rampart, through the winding street, past the colonnade, between the crowds which opened, and into the piazza at last to the tall lady. The one and the other walked quickly and with single purpose, hair blowing, one official and one man walking as if they might not reach the gallows after all. The prisoner's greatcoat was open and it beat about his ankles; he walked now, came foot to stone.

And then there was no further for him to walk. The two of us stepped to the center of the trap, that board which shall be fastened so that it be firm at the proper time and fail at the proper time, leaving the foot nothing but emptiness. The muscles at the corners of the prisoner's mouth were hard like welts. There was not a minute more. He made a gesture as if to remove the greatcoat. But I bound his wrists, strapped the ankles, pulling the thongs tight. I put the hood upon him, down over the ears. I lifted the noose—higher, with both hands, lifting—and fixed it more easily than I dreamed. Then he stepped off the trap.

And that one noise of machine and man echoed and rebounded against the four sides of the piazza, against the campanile and the low tower, and disappeared down my winding road. Then in the silence the trap banged several times like a door. I stood at the edge of the pit where the rope before me descended quiet and taut, tugged steady as some line dropped through a hole into the center of the earth.

And in the crowd, back near the wall, I saw Antonina. Already her hair was gray and her complexion altered, the lips compressed, the temples shiny, and her habits and her character so true and poorly tempered that no man would come for her and the rest of her days would be spent with the manual for the virgins not yet released to marriage.

And then there was the air damp and cold and the owl exerting himself into flight, beating through the top branches now, shutting his eyes and crashing through the twigs to the dripping hole in the trunk, settling himself and sitting inside the bark for summers and winters, and he stayed thus, peering out of the warmth, the tenure of silent feathers in a cold tree.

Thus stands the cause between us, we are entered into covenant for this work, we have drawn our own articles and have professed to enterprise upon these actions and these ends, and we have besought favor, and we have bestowed blessing.

The Goose on the Grave

One must have resonance, resonance and sonority…like a goose.

Homage to Sextus Propertius

EZRA POUND

1

The priests on three white donkeys descended from a cloud and down the walls came into the steeper end of Castiglione's city. The beasts were for once unsure of footing and without a halt turned their white heads toward the top while little black pointed boots laced furtively into the shorthaired flanks. The blackbreasts made a single file, one above the other, tightly skirted and silent, sunken into the end of a dusty journey. Chains were disarranged at their sides, the riders having been stopped far back on the road by thieves. These heavenly picadors now stuck against the white roof of the city; then turned, high as the bell tower, and without pity picked over the tiles below. Down there moved the decked-out sinners, beating across smokeless chimneys. The priests arrived from over the mountains to the toning of the morning call.

Under the sign of the winged cock chopped in relief from the door arch, butting its broken stone-tip out of antiquity, the dismounted priests made their own sign: against the past's brazen statuary, against the secret parts of the dead hung from the house walls like abnormalities perpetrated upon the loins of faceless cherubin with the power of flight. The stone was pink, the salmon color of long inactivity, out of which dropped the gray heraldry of half the populace, the hindward spectacle of meeting dogs.

In went the priests. Striking the door, they stepped to the side of Adeppi's mother. Adeppi, sitting in the darkness with the scattered litter of his brothers and sisters crying upward from the floor, watched them cross, lift, and carry her off.

The donkeys stepped out gamely with the load slung between and again picked their way up the steep, nosing the shaggy thighs of strangers.

Adeppi remained for a time where he was, kneeling and silent. Dust and the upflung sheets settled again to the bed; he heard the children fall about each other. Adeppi, one of Italy's covey of fragile doves, rose, stole out to the sunlight and in the opposite direction from the donkeys, ran down over the heated stones despite the cries that followed from the mouth of the abandoned cave.

A bakery and a hospital joined at the end of a narrow street blocked with carts upon which casualties lay in the sunlight. Ovens and operating benches merged beyond lakeblue plaster walls. Adeppi smelled the still wet antiseptic blankets and the rising loaves. He sat on the hospital steps and watched the puttees green with mold passing up and down. The litters rolled to the gait of the boots scratching the dust and the flattened twigs spilled in the road. His haunches cooled on the stone and the sun fell across his back. From the darkness behind, Adeppi heard the ringing of bloody pans. At an angle to himself the baker's women came one at a time to the doorway, peered into the sky and at the slow movement of the injured into the Ospedale.

During the state's year of dissolution, the chains across the city gates were smashed and smoke rolled in from the sea and across the mountains. Hardly awake, the baker's women in the morning brushed flour from their bosoms, out of their hair, and the white sack dresses bagged slackly over nakedness. The dough they pulled in the daytime soured at night, but another day blossomed in the starving kilns. The pure brown flour itself was smoothed as between palms in near empty, mill sweet bins, smelled faintly by the citizens as it drifted from the baker's whitewashed chimney. Adeppi's mouth was dry.

Two men entered the iron-patched yard of the church—its nave was filled with the wounded—and stooped to the weight of the stretcher they carried with handles across their shoulders, like an African queen carried on humps nearly drained of water; they stopped at the smooth blocks rising toward stained glass. Unable to climb further, the one in front slipped from under his load, rested the end of the stretcher on the stones.

He began to smoke while the rear bearer stood in traces, arms pulled toward the ground by the sway of human gravity.

Adeppi crept close to the soldier who lay on his back fixedly staring into the sun. Nino had been sick on the blankets packed thickly and drawn close about his wounded neck. Adeppi shaded the eyes with his hand. The first carrier turned around, snuffling the cigarette on his puttee, and watched the boy breathe into the severed face. Then from his belt the carrier unhooked a heart-shaped water bottle and leaned forward, at the same time pulling at his bandanna with which to wipe the drinker's mouth. Adeppi saw the water splash and a few drops roll from flesh to cloth; and the tongue, greedy, unconscious of pain, dart suddenly and glide across the lips. He heard the loaves pushed from the baker's window on a board to cool. When they started again, he followed. Holding to the edge of the stretcher, his fingers caught below the blanket, Adeppi trailed into the cool darkness and asked for his mother.

Three priests turned and hid behind the altar.

This stretcher was propped on two saw horses, and he stood beside it in the dark. An officer at the head of the stretcher, another stooping over the middle, pulled the blankets from the soldier. With razors they cut away one of the green legs of the britches. Adeppi looked at the brown limb, clothed on top, booted on the bottom, and looked down the rows of men settled on the floor. The knife slit harmlessly, without sound, across the leg. And the other way, in the direction of a cross, burning a

thin line down the skin. Adeppi reached out his hand
and touched the unfamiliar warm flatness of the thigh,
for only a moment, as if both hands had come against
the breast of a fallen animal in a ditch, his own feet bare
and ankle deep in roadside water. The sun issued evenly
from the flesh under his hand. But, frightened, he looked
at the doctor and quickly pulled his fingers away, lest
they too fall beneath the blade.

"Little boy," a voice echoed from the farthest soldier
quietly bedridden on the stone, "sing for us!"

Adeppi had come into the world's platoon of broken
lances and even while he smelled the iodine, he heard
the far-off cries of women as the hot crusts burned their
palms.

When they blew out the light, he crept from soldier
to soldier, sitting cross-legged between the bodies. Behind the church the sky turned pale with darkness, lu-
minously blue beyond the balconies, and the cypress in
the graveyard glistened, as did the steeple.

Seville, Venezia, the voice of sunken cities and for
the love of a woman—he tasted the first few notes and
the chin lifted, feeling for the octave like a gypsy reaching out, upward on his mandolin, marking time in the
air. Still Adeppi could not sing. Nino watched him
sharply, kept him close by, and waited for the shrill notes
to ring with the bells. Nino was finally able to use his
leg, though the wound on his neck was unhealed and a
gradual swelling gave him pain. He did not rejoin his
regiment. Instead he stayed about the hospital. The
months were fragrant and a few grapes behind the hos-

pital on the graveyard vines began to twitch in the heat.

Nino took Adeppi with him at night. Soldier and boy sat under the partially bearing vines. They did not speak, but Nino tried to sing while Adeppi watched the movement of the lips. Laughter came from the bakery, the slapping of fists into bags of flour. But from the castle-shaped heights of the city, not a head peered down. Nino could not carry a tune, yet snatches of slow song, on a terrible raw voice, continued to the patient beat of the soldier's finger. Adeppi learned these songs from him who, with puffy throat, low soft teeth and curling hair, throwing out his chest, sang with hampered rumbling desire. In the middle he would break off himself and finish the song by the waving of a finger, shaking it at the boy.

There was wine as well as bread in the bakery. For weeks Nino visited there, going just at dusk and returning before dark. On these visits he drank with Edouard and did not speak to the white-smocked girls. The first time Nino brought Adeppi, Edouard met them at the door. There was straw hanging above Edouard's head, a feather dried to the stone and cobweb. He smiled as one smiles from a ruin in the evening, a particular pleasure in spying a church window on the edge of a place of hiding and at dusk. Egg scavengers, thought Edouard, are climbing through the rubble in the condemned fields, making for, lifting their eyes toward, the same golden dome.

Hand in hand they stood in the yard. Adeppi held his cap tightly. A starving guinea hen perched on the rim of the hooded sealed well, the setting sun streaked across the clay. Outside man and boy stood in the shadow of ancient buttresses.

"Older than you think, Padrone," Nino murmured. Without waiting for an answer, he slid forward and squeezed past Edouard into the cool, wood-smelling darkness.

Edouard searched the cupboards and after a time put a liter of wine on the table. Adeppi smelled the heat dying from the ovens beyond the wall. The three sat without a light.

"Shall we leave the shutters open or shut? Shut them." Edouard sat down.

"Salute," said Nino. He leaned forward with both arms on the table. Watching Edouard, he closed one eye and drew down the eyebrow, wrinkling the cheek. Still Edouard would not notice the boy. The bandage around his neck began to throb. He clasped his hands and, with two stubby fingers together built a steeple to amuse Adeppi, then collapsed it. He wiped his mouth on his sleeve.

Edouard looked at him. "Five," he whispered, "each with a petticoat." He reached across the table and clapped Adeppi on the shoulder. Nino's long hair curled into his eyes.

Finally Edouard lit a lantern, and picked it up. The two men discovered that Adeppi had left the table. They saw him, barefooted, small, crouched at the door that led upstairs, his nose and staring eyes pressed into the jamb. Edouard, twirling the lamp, turned to Nino.

"Flagrante delicto!" he said softly and laughed. He began to whisper.

"Not tonight," shouted Nino. And then carelessly: "The boy," he added, "it's time he went to bed."

They did not enter the hospital but sat on the steps where they first met. They watched the dew that had started from the stone. Windows were quiet behind their wooden mantles.

"After a minute," Nino patted the boy's head, "we'll go back."

Adeppi could not speak; he clutched at Nino's trousers.

"Wait," Nino smiled broadly. "A minute yet, ragazzo."

He kept a steady watch on the bakery, smoked quickly. Once he stole into the hospital and returned, knowing well the supply chests, with a fresh wad of cotton stuffed in the bandage about his neck. Again he took Adeppi's hand and they crossed the few paces of moonlit square. As they walked, Adeppi pulled and the soldier held him tightly.

Nino robbed Edouard of his guitar. With a hand clapped over Adeppi's mouth, holding the boy noiselessly off the floor, he crept back into the room where they had drunk wine and lifted the guitar from its peg on the wall. Outside, he slipped the cord over his neck, regardless of the wound, and as he walked the instrument hit his side. Unstrummed, it issued a hollow sound.

No one saw them. In front of the bakery, close to the shadow, Nino struck his feet far apart and caught Adeppi by the collar. He positioned the guitar. Then, with a jerk of the wrist, he swung the boy to his shoulder. Frowning, with only one hand, Nino began pecking out a song. He said nothing, but he squeezed the child's legs and watched the window.

Adeppi threw back his head and suddenly drove his fingers into Nino's hair. He swayed from the shoulder as a mad bird on a perch. The soprano voice, through one song after another, soared and the lungs puffed under the chin, the clear notes pained his nostrils. There was the lapping of waters, dark, flowing between the house of love and the Ponte Beffa, a cape skirled in an archway. Adeppi's eyes were wide, his tongue darted, he too watched the window.

It creaked when it opened. He lifted his hand, slowly, to his rising voice, shifting under the arm braced across his knees, and saw the dim shaggy head of hair. He screamed from his egg-shaped mouth, stood up, reaching for the window.

She listened for a moment, leaned out, lowering the gown. Then softly, her voice audible despite his cry, she said with a quickening: "Avanti! Avanti!" and withdrew.

Boy and guitar were flung to the ground.

The next time Adeppi sings the room is full, well lit by lamps. Edouard, seated with knees close together, holds the guitar, its great frog-like dusty bell rolling in his lap. He watches Adeppi. All of them listen, the five women, the men with heavily sunburnt lips, and Nino.

Nino holds the woman he courted so craftily on his lap and runs his finger over the cool inside of her thigh.

No longer does he have to speak at all. His bandage is discarded; the woman's hair comes down upon his shoulder.

There is the smell of tomato over the urn of ashes. They have called Adeppi and he stands in short pants cut off high near the top of his legs, and no shirt. Stocky shoulders are held back, firm, hands in fists are at his side. And his shaved olive head is pointed at the rafters, his face alone works with the effort of the muscles around his gullet and moistened lips. Grown fat, smaller, isolated in a glaze of medieval lyricism, sweating and working at the song, he forces himself to voice those ecstatic melodies to which so many countesses have met and sinned, so many wolfhounds bayed.

For the exit of a few batteries of cannon, officials dropped the chains that pinched off the leathery slopes of the city. Adeppi was there with the rest to wave his cap at the passing of the guns that were ridden, like land-impaled porpoises, by the artillerymen whose torn trousers flapped astraddle the iron of the breeches. The powder-borne weapons heaved slowly to the south. Clanking, the mauled unit passed, the black-burned naked heels of the soldiers striking like tin against the sides of downward aiming guns. Several times a day Adeppi came out of the shade to watch, back down the winding open stairways when he heard the crash of chains. Then he was gone again, trilling in Castiglione's town houses and drawing up to those who smelled of smoke.

He climbed the town's vertical walls alone. At the

fountain the water carriers smiled at him as their shawls swung in the dust, and they held first one bucket then another heavily against their breasts and under the spout. At the foot of the campanile, outside the coffin maker's shop, or under the window where the countess toileted, at these places he stood sentry amid the rumbling of the carts and sang, the fishlike outline of his mouth wide open in his sunburnt face. He napped under a madonna's head that stared from a sun-streaked wall at the harness of donkeys and a clear sky filled with the shot of hovering birds. Nino's wounds had healed; the guitar warped on its peg.

Adeppi preferred the crowds, the old women who never drank twice at the fountain, each one of whom had borne two soldiers, one thief, and a daughter in Rome. They plucked at the skirts of priests and bled under the fruit trees by the grave, now shaking their own skirts, leading nameless passersby to the rooms of venery. When he followed, the old women turned agilely about and shook the black skirts between their hidden legs. And he would hide in the recess of a wall and count the coins that had been tossed him.

He peered into sleeping rooms that opened upon the cobblestones without the shield of hallway or antechamber, in view of all who walked. In the evening he found his own voice drowned by the church's choir. Heat issued from his body as it had from Nino's leg and once, in the noon crowd, he was hugged quickly and heavily by a woman who picked up the basket she had dropped and disappeared before he could see her face. A moment later three priests passed, dragging after them asses with heads outstretched on the ends of jerking bridles.

To other children, loitering on the steps of the governor's palace, he sang snatches of the songs with which, later in the hot night, he quieted babies carried aimlessly by night mothers or set out amid empty demijohns on the brown balconies. The darkness itself labored up the steep landings and incline of the city, or fell swiftly down the tiles which, held without mortar, dropped through the night their sound of breaking porcelain—phantom vandals darting at the pedestal of a saint.

One night, having sung to the coffin maker asleep over his boards, having passed on to wander in the women's portion of the town, catching them as they opened or shut a door, tired and cramped in a dream, Adeppi returned to the bakery. A hundred steps from the entrance he stopped. Then, stooping double, he shoved his coins beneath the belly of a weather-beaten sheep that lay in the rotten straw of a crèche inside the wall.

Edouard blocked the door and, in the darkness, leaned forward and braced his hands on his fat thighs, so that his face was on a level with the boy's. He squatted, listening with another sense to the night gossip through the grillwork and, wide-awake, would have a good deal to tell his intimates by morning.

"I've been waiting for you," Edouard whispered, "I've been waiting for you to come back."

Adeppi put his foot on the stair and climbed into a light smoking overhead. The chalkstone was cool and smooth, the narrow shaft filled with the odor of leavening. A few dried bulbs and herbs bristled thinly, the women came from their rooms to watch.

"Maria," they whispered, "be kind to him!"

In this close hallway under the eaves, Adeppi found Nino helpless, dressed only in his army tunic, tight, shrunken. It did not cover his waist. Out of reach, her hair loosed, trembling with laughter, stood Bianca Maria. Her back bent against the low beams.

Edouard peered over the women's heads.

"Edouard," they cried, "Edouard, cover him up!"

Nino struck a liter, empty and yellow, and it rolled away to return rattling to the tilt of the floor and lodge against his ribs. He looked straight at Edouard and the boy and cleared his throat. "Bianca Maria, your hand." It was a loud croak, Adeppi saw movement in the scar under the jawbone, and the woman shook her head happily, pressing backward a step. Nino was affixed to the floor; they stood over him with a lantern shining on his black-haired haunches.

"Maria, only your hand," whispered Nino.

Below his knee, in the thick of his calf, was the declivity of his second wound, the flesh white and pinched unevenly as if it had been sawed from the tooth of a wild hog. Edouard looked at the scar, then, taking breath, gazed at the waiting girl whose fingers played with the hanging firewood that turned into acrid smoke.

The soldier began, without smiling and in monotone, to imitate the song that Adeppi had sung beneath her window. And, with a single energy, he lifted his hand from the floor, suspended it limply without support, outstretched from his body in hypnotic endurance, so that those who watched leaned forward, feeling the heaviness of flesh and bone and the tingling in the fingertips.

"Dopo, dopo," Maria whispered over and over, seriously and with feeling, as if she did not want Edouard to hear.

"Take his hand," he said, slipping among the women, and slowly, face averted, Adeppi obeyed. He sat cross-legged, his fat brown chest perspiring. "Quick!" urged Edouard, and reaching up, the boy took hold of the soldier's hand and slowly drew it to his lap. Maria watched him closely.

Nino shut his eyes, rolling his head.

Edouard pressed a Florentine florin into Adeppi's other hand.

The children are at the windows late in the night, peering into dry canals and at frescoes flaking on Roman walls. These sleepers cry for food over the roofs of lava, mothers roll and thrust away the child. In the streets the beggar thrusts the bottom of his foot toward the moon. Cats cross now on the Bridge of Straw.

Leaning out of the narrow window in the sunlight, Adeppi rubbed his fingers in his shorn scalp, watched a motor ambulance fit itself into the entrance to the court. Then he drank a cup of warm water and went down to the well yard below. The guinea hen thrust her scaled head into the sun bright on the handcart-rutted clay, and the women dipped the buckets one by one from the well. Black hair was uncombed, their working smocks spotted from the dampness of the stones. One was pregnant, and she too smoked and talked of the night that had just passed. Adeppi sat on the rim of the well and watched their faces that had faded in the darkness until now, as they wiped water from their eyes with sackcloth, a sleepy belligerence lay on the flesh and they were older. Around the windlass and mended rope they talked like men and, pulling up the flat skirts, felt at bruises on their upper legs.

Stone and plaster, white mortar, tile and slate, crumbling, slowly the backs of the houses emerged from shadow and sweated in the sun. The women dropped their cigarettes down the well and prepared to work. Pale thin strings of smoke rose from the enormous chimneys, as a handful of twigs curled in small iron burners on the hearths.

They were milling in the yard, the child's face as expressionless as the women's, when Nino appeared in the doorway followed by the crashing of his boots. Below his tunic, still without trousers, he wore a short canvas undergarment, hastily tied. In his hand he waved a pistol, not a military firearm but an old weapon come by illegally, once the possession of a noblewoman. The guinea hen dashed behind a pile of manure.

Nino ran straight to Adeppi. The soldier did not touch him, did not put a hand on his arm, but placed the muzzle against the boy's temple. The gun was steady.

The women shouted for Edouard.

"Stop the noise," commanded Nino. The pistol was pressing against Adeppi's ear, he stared ahead shamefully, bewildered. Still aiming the gun, delicate, menacing, Nino began to rub his flat jaw. Absently, he opened the tunic.

Had the short scarred finger pulled the trigger, there would have been a flash, a leaping of the silver gun in the air, and a sharp noise echoing away among the ruins. The shot would have crossed the ancient tiles and disappeared. Nino's wild figure stood quivering by the hooded well, his feet deep in the dust, and at that moment the blast of the bullet would not have come unexpectedly: a man so excited in the early morning, clad only partially in a uniform, could have killed and not disturbed the early puttering of the old peasants in their yards.

Then, as if trying to remember, Nino laid the pistol on the well rim beside the boy. A worn medallion hung outside his tunic. He fingered it and his left eye closed narrowly.

"Nino, come up here, Nino." An early morning breeze swept Edouard's blond curls.

The women waited as the soldier walked slowly, buttoning his coat. Then they too trailed off to work, smiling. The pistol splashed down the well.

Adeppi pushed it, a quick movement, and it was gone. All morning he stayed in the silent yard. He wandered about the low walls as if waiting for Nino to come at him again, or sat crouched in the doorway. Several times he worked with the rope and bucket, trying to retrieve the gun. He remembered the nights he had sat beneath the trees with Nino and explored the soldier's kit.

Once he called out, but there was no answer. Only the hidden women kneading loudly. The sun rose higher, white on the moistened roofs, teeming across the airless turrets, and, as the day filled with noise, Adeppi felt more and more alone, confined to the sheltered yard. But as he waited, there came, not from the second floor but from the third, up under the roof, the light whine of the guitar, and voices, in unison, attempting to sing above their laughter.

At noon, sobered, Nino reappeared with all his bags and equipment. His trench knife was in place, his thick britches wrapped neatly in puttees.

"I'm going," he announced. "Adeppi, wish me luck."

They shook hands. "Arrivederci," said Adeppi and bowed. He stepped back and watched Nino fastening himself with straps. And, for the first time that morning, to see him off, Bianca Maria came into the yard. She wore a gray spangled dress, no stockings, no jewelry. She smoothed the sides of her skirt and kept glancing at the angle of the sun, constantly walking and with only a quick smile for Adeppi. Now and then Nino looked up to admire her.

From his soldier's great roll of musty gear, he pulled a large wooden camera, a tacked-down box that had a slowshutting, enormous lens. He held it in front of his face and peered through the slot, stepping in blind, artistic half-circles. Fumbling, he pushed forward toward the girl who faced him now, motionless, in the sunlight. Adeppi stood behind her and to one side, leaning against the wall. Maria looked over her shoulder.

"Adeppi, come. Be in the picture." He shook his head.

Nino braced the camera against his chest. Bianca Maria posed with her eyes toward the stork-nested chimneys, with her hands to her throat, and once on her knees clutching the old guinea hen to her breast. She drew closer and closer to the photographer. Nino said nothing, perspiring in his heavy uniform. Adeppi could see nothing of the girl's face, her back was to him, knew nothing of the expression, color, or contour that met the opening lens.

Then, squarely in front of the camera, she stooped and lightly caught up the hem of her dress for the departing soldier, and drew the front of it above her waist. The skirt hung like parted wings on the dusty air. Through the transparency of the single thickness, Adeppi saw the outline of her legs.

"Goodbye, goodbye," called Nino as she ran into the bakery. "Walk with me to the street," he said to Adeppi and, the army straps in place and all his belongings tied across his back, they started sadly toward the gate.

They parted in the middle of the road that climbed straight up from the village and descended swiftly to the low country. A few old men and women, from their perches in the walls, watched the two separate: Nino upward leaning on his staff like a pike, Adeppi downward. Nino, unshaven and stiff, carried his rootless treasures to the distant fields. The episode of the pistol dis-

appeared into the youth of the street singer, but, thereafter, while he counted upon the return of his companion, he was armed.

"Arrivederci!"

There was a corner on which Adeppi liked to stand;
and it was to this spot that he ran, pushing through a
caravan of children in slouch hats and ragged shirts. The
Bocca di Piazza, often empty, was overhung with the
blades of shops and littered with silent baskets from
which the doves had been sold for sacrifice. Now it was
full with silent forms squeezed one by one through the
seven-foot arch as if some secret ceremony had ended.
Bright scarves fluttered about the dark heads; there was
no weight to the parcels on their backs. Slowly they
entered and left the square, while those who had gained
the center milled, knocking against craven stones. Across
the piazza on the steps of the boarded-up opera house
small boys fought with folding knives.

This was the silent portion of the city—Adeppi remembered the sudden gesture of the woman and the
skirt against his mouth—and he found his way around
three sides of the piazza before he discovered once more
the exact spot where, under the eyes of the small
madonna who gazed upon the harness of ghostly burros, he liked to stop. Adeppi leaned against the head of
a gargoyle with a ring in its teeth. The strange crowd
grew heavier.

The madonna was unusually small, a wooden figurine
in a box covered with broken glass. Her colors were
faded. But the woodcarver had made up for the small

size by excessive clothing; two eastern cloaks and a heavy sash wrapped her around, thick crude wooden creases obscured the chin and the feet. The madonna peered fiercely from this weight, suffering in the sunlight. Mysteriously burdened, she gazed with enamel face across the city and held up her empty arms. The thick skirt and wear of the weather hid nothing, the woodcarver had sculptured his madonna still with child, to look down on this square of small boys.

Adeppi looked up at the wind-beaten statue. The sun tinted the cowl and few spikes of the halo, a worn-down eightday candle burned invisibly in the light. One of the crowd paused behind him and with an arm reaching over his head, dropped a coin against the madonna's pedestal. Before Adeppi could move, the hand, withdrawing, knocked him on the ear. He heard the rattle of musket and heavy bayonet, and Nino disappeared into the stream, for a moment tipping his rifle in salute.

2

At the Caffè Gatto, Edouard leaned forward and kissed the top of an old man's head pitted in the crook of his arm. The old fellow's free hand swung out. But the primo camiere had already drawn back and was untouched. The crier whispered it was midnight.

"Giovinastro!" shouted the drinkers. Edouard wet his lips and, glancing over the room, kept his eye some few inches higher than the heads of the tallest dancing men. Now and then he stepped from the box hidden behind the bar, bent double to rinse a glass in the bucket of green water at his feet. He was dressed for night: a shirt without sleeves or collar, a red tie around the neck, and a black band on the forearm. The back of his skull, reflected in the white framed mirror, was sharp, a piece of Roman stone. Around the mirror were pasted photographs of sallow men in straw hats. And Edouard's own picture was among them. Leaves of mercury discolored the glass.

"Edouard, the cat, Signorina, I am he, beautiful Signorina. I have a tail," he told women who visited the Gatto for the first time, having come perhaps from Umberto's sleeping chamber. On the opposite wall was a portrait of two enormous Siamese cats, painted close together, one atop the other, conveying the heat climbing upon the night, and the two faces seemed to be pressed into a single growth of whiskers, too starved to fight. There were no other cats in the Gatto; only the sardines which Edouard lately placed on every table, the smell of cat hairs on the wood, the archness of the dancers' feet.

Edouard took another sip of the vermouth. His chest itched as if it were covered with hair. Jacopo watched him.

"Basta, basta," muttered Adeppi but Jacopo only stretched his accordion again, until it had taken a full breath, and played. He leaned back, crossed his ankles, and watched Edouard. Adeppi took a breath and again sang "La Gelosia." He walked a few paces, put his hand on a table, a few more paces and stopped again. His voice was louder than the accordion, shrill. He pushed through the dancers. When he came near the bar, Edouard looked at his watch. "Another hour, ragazzo." He laughed and put a coin within reach.

Adeppi did not answer him but put the soldi in his pocket and loudly made his way back to Jacopo, squatted and sang at the accordionist's feet.

"Pussy cat, pussy cat, Jacopo," Edouard called.

Jacopo turned the bellows of the accordion in his direction and peered darkly over the top of the instrument, dropping many notes from the music. Again he looked to the bar.

"Get up," he said, "Edouard wants you to walk around."

For a moment the accordion choked. Jacopo concentrated on seeing Edouard, all of him—the yellow and black hair, the whiteness in the eye, the sharp fall of the shoulders, and behind him the straw hats. On opposite sides of the room, Jacopo and Edouard faced each other and did not move. But the accordion followed the provveditore, though Jacopo held it tightly about the throat, and repeated "La Gelosia" over and over in the rhythm of a death march.

Jacopo wore a short gray jacket on his shoulders—it had begun to rot the summer before—and from his ears, cut into the lobes, hung two square crystal earrings that once belonged to the women of his family. He had a habit of sticking out his tongue, though his fixed eyes forbade that strangers laugh or smile at him.

Edouard twisted the end of the red tie in his fingers. He waited. Suddenly he tucked it into his shirt and picked up the glass in both trembling hands, saluted Jacopo, drank. The vermouth smelled of cold skin.

Around him the young men ate cheese and eggs in the late night, but they did not bother to glance at the singer over their forks. Adeppi, the color of a fried fish, moved among the tables. For a moment he heard

Edouard gaily humming the song behind him. Edouard never tired; he trimmed the hair out of his nostrils at sunrise and then slept.

Jacopo clapped the accordion in and out, pushed the stops on the pipe organ of the continent. His tongue was pointed. He had danced with Edouard in Brussels. In an Alsatian cemetery he had played his accordion softly for the burial of Edouard's first partner, a dwarf. He had come down with fever soon after Edouard in Trieste. Both of them had been found in the waters off Marseilles and taken for dead. But, one spring, they had ridden through the center of Berlin in a black hansom, before Edouard dyed his hair and before he himself grew thin. Now they were without fortune; he dreamt of Edouard's face, Edouard standing with cane and straw hat, Edouard throwing him a coin in Il Valentino.

Adeppi's forehead was wet, his feet bare and flat. Jacopo waved him away; he stood against the white wall, the music heavy upon his chest, his hands automatically pulling at the wooden keys. Air hissed from the pasteboard bellows. Now Edouard was motioning, suddenly flicking his wrist above the heads. He was old for such a worried smile. Jacopo began to play a waltz, watched through half-closed eyes to see the change on Edouard's face. For his own part, nothing could be different: he remembered Edouard describing frescoes that depicted the creation of the world, and he was unmoved. His arms hugged the song, but in a cold catacomb he watched to see Edouard's collapse.

"Edouard has changed his mind," whispered Adeppi.

Jacopo nodded. He rested his head against the wall. For a moment the music, though reedy, was anticipative, preoccupied. However, he continued immediately with a polka. The dancers struck shoulder to shoulder.

"Ciao, ciao," bowed Edouard. And if he saw a strange face: "Psst, what is your name, Giovenco?"

Jacopo played another stanza. "Plauso! Plauso!" exclaimed Edouard, rising as of old. He clapped his hands. At his soft enthusiastic shout, the dancers stirred uneasily and glanced at the quick brutal cats on the wall. Jacopo refused to finish the song; he was not convinced when the man called himself a grand "provveditore" and vigorously shook a glass which he had pulled from the dirty pail. Jacopo stuck out his tongue; Edouard despised the sight of it. The accordionist pressed his fingers down, the screws were falling from his accordion. People talked to the sound of his music—Adeppi's singing made them talk with their hands, catch each other's hands in exclamation—and the metallic passages seemed to liven their white faces like a Viennese orchestra, turned the caffè, the park, or the blind street into a garden of buried remonstrance and love song. Alone, hair faded at the temples, Jacopo was central Europe's aged violinist among empty tables. He was not of the crowd—thinking, plotting, remembering behind the smoke and the beckoning of the instrument—a worn, thinned, narrow-eyed renderer of wine cellar music.

Edouard slipped through a side door to the alley behind the Gatto. He took a candle with him. On moonless nights, in village after village, the accordionist had seen him shielding a precarious pure candle rigidly over the undrained stones, quickly lest the insects come to it. He returned. The wick was red. He was shivering, no match for the night clouds, the flacons of the canal, the tread of lonely boots. He poured a small bit of brandy into his glass.

The old man woke. His face, covered with spittle, turned slowly up from the bar. With a sudden flattening move he caught the end of Edouard's tie. Head on its side, the old man grimaced. His arm retracted steadily bit by bit and slowly pulled the provveditore close. They stared with horror into each other's eyes. The dancers, pair by pair, stood still.

"Discrezione, discrezione!" whispered Edouard sternly, trying to loose the red knot. "I beg you…" He choked and pretended to cough behind the back of his hand. Jacopo was out of tune. "Really. I must insist…" and the whisper glided up, inaudible. The arm jerked, the head responded uncomfortably.

"Oh, ah, keep them apart, shame," murmured the dancers softly. They stood on their toes. The accordion was conscious only of its own chromatic preoccupation, its blinded chords.

Edouard's eyes grew paler each year and now, wishing no help, he tried to hide their starting from the watery sockets. His raucous, excited breathing pained his own ears. With effort, reddening despite the blood already stopped in his head, he raised his arm fitfully and began, not as smoothly as he might, to stroke the other's wrist. He attempted to turn himself away from the crowd and toward the mirror, the photograph. Best wishes to Edouard. "You will…wrinkle my tie," he managed to whisper at last.

"Bah! You mostro!" shouted the old man and, falling from his stool, fled, knocking them aside.

Edouard panted. Then he smiled and motioned with both hands up as if to reassure them. He took three deep breaths. And, exuberantly, he caught the street singer in his arms and swung him off the floor.

"Bimbo," he laughed in relief, "bimbo, bimbo," and hugged the boy from side to side, swinging the bare feet. He was dancing himself, breathing through his mouth.

Jacopo slipped from the black straps, rested the accordion against the wall. His shoulders ached.

Edouard

He found himself early in the century. It was of a sudden, in an Emperor's garden a few moments after it was opened to the public that afternoon, when, looking up from some children romping stiffly, he saw a rider astride a horse with rump broad in the fashion of those times and tail grotesquely bobbed above it; the horse, the sportsman, the plunderous hooves appearing heavy and uncertain on the fresh path, the beast walking like a dray in livery to the fretful ticking of the chopped and twisted stump of jet tail. This mammoth apparition passed but a few steps away, stirred up the earth after the morning's shower, and shook the blossoms of the peach trees immediately over Edouard's head. The rider hesitated, then reined his animal and kept its threatening hind legs from splashing Edouard's checkered trousers, as if in a glance he had thought better of muddying one who avoided stepping on the golden fruit at his feet.

Long and triumphantly he remembered the decisive moment when the horseman gave his signal, mysterious, with knees, wrists, or whatever, remembered the Black turn submissive at the coaxing of its master—count or chevalier—and pass, its staggering rear crowned by the tail in crupper gone at last into the misty horizon of the garden, the pink and green. Distinctly, the horse had bowed to him.

And the horse, prancing and light boned or barrel-buttocked, sightless in black blinders, or breasting the fog with red eye, became the animal he too could ride so far forward on the withers in tailored uniform or make lift her front legs with one hefty loop of his stinging whip. Carriage horses, stock horses of Belgian soldiers, fillies and colts slim in starvation, there were mounts for Edouard across Europe's glittering paddock and slyly he fed sugar from a yellow glove to the four-legged pedigreed denizens out of Arabia.

He introduced himself as a horse trainer, he took his walks where the best of the breed paraded, and grew to know this all-curried and handsomely saddled world of pleasure by the colors of nearby stables. At one time his favorite was a purple stallion, at another a homely sorrel ridden by a lady in a veil and small black boots, and again he admired a pony kicking its groom. He dreamed of a fortunate trio of whites dancing round and round a pavilion filled with the smell of sawdust and roses and the brass trumpeting of a Netherlandish orchestra. The horse was his aristocrat, their belly bands were cummerbunds of rank, and to the height of his early career they practiced their five gaits each afternoon before his keen sense of form and flesh, and he met well, received well, patted his luck at arm's length, and got about the city well without ever trusting himself to the saddle. Still, he had hoped one day to return to the Emperor's garden seated upon a horse. And had failed.

Now there was only the horse fly. The stall was in ruin. Outside the caffè, testing himself tentatively against the wall, there was not much to ask of the night or of the flies at his neck again. And the candle, the piece of glass, the disappearing soap cake secreted in an iron hand grip—he suspected street children of using it behind his back—all were nothing compared with the silver brush upon whose curve a fox and "Edouard" had been engraved. Then stolen. He was wearing his nightcoat, holding it aside.

Blood fell on the newspaper. His shoelaces would become too wet again to dry by morning. Returning, how the guards' horses—small, dusty, ribbed—had shamed him at the gates of Vatican City, and how the horse flies had shamed him there, finding him so readily, settling upon him with such familiarity, Italian, as if smelling at once a friend with sweeter sugar and horse hair on his jacket. His country's domes, the Venite, the avenues with troughs used only by birds and children, were reduced to a constant recollection of dysentery.

Long had he been driven back to the country of flies like blue ticks, thrown back perhaps only hours before the Grand Steeplechase, as neatly as if he had been tossed off into a muddy ditch. He brought with him a pair of opera glasses for the field and Jacopo who was no equestrian. The old world took the bit in her teeth and stood still like an ass. He was accustomed now to the toilet in the street and waited for the buzzing to approach, grow loud, and become a sudden irritant feasting with mouth full between his neck and collar.

But he still donned his striped trousers to cross from the bakery to the Caffè Gatto, now pausing—an eternal cheapside pause—before setting off for the church's spot of feasting. He was in search of the red Riviera, how long it was since they had been to the Turkish baths or cycled together through Balkan capitals. And they had been detained at that last entrance, inoculated on the outermost docks in sight of Naples with its beds of contagious seaweed, as if the two of them were old parrots carrying some tropical disease. Though since landing, they had not been entirely without their flirting with amusement—until the country had nothing more to offer.

The flies walked up and down his nightcoat. He bled, drop by drop; it was late and here he stood, hanging to the handgrips in an iron lady, apparatus of shield and spikes. He was plagued by the ghosts of small and famous jockeys, heard their dim bowlegged steps through the weeds at night.

"Jacopo, is it you?" He looked straight up at a shadow wide as the round head of Il Duomo, and beyond it into the stars lumining the grave's end, wrapping a few fretful saints. Then he peered over his shoulder. "Watch where you step," he murmured and saw the earrings sparkle.

Suddenly his left hand was torn from the grip, as by a pump sucking irascibly its wreckage, and thrown back against the tin; he was turned half around by his shoulder, drawing to the corner, waiting, wishing to close the nightcoat. There was hardly room for two. With dismal anticipation, he hoped he would not fall on his face.

"Jacopo," hazarding, "have you forgotten the Palazzo Pesaro?"

Perhaps in the days to come, he could pay the child to unclog the drain. For surely his footing would be lost and he would be left to lie in the water. "I hope," it was hard to talk, "you haven't ... lost my soap...."

He concluded after some minutes—vaguely the thoughts rattled about inside his head—that since Jacopo hit him with the upperside rather than the underside of the hand, it was the nails he felt on his cheek and their stinging that remained when the arm swept each time to the end of its half circle in the dark. It was true, his eyes did flash, and at one of the more painful blows—it grazed his eyelids—he took heart because he loved color. And now the light of his own paining pupils ran up and down the lavatory walls, quickening with red and silver the sweaty iron. He could see the place and realized that when struck, former sights were driven from the eyes, jarred from the walls of the retina unexpectedly, loosed to swim perversely down the system of optics in brilliant discoloration. From his left eye, beaten but still open, he saw Jacopo without benefit of the narcotic colors: only close, too close, and he allowed it to shut in the swelling grown like a compress upon his cheekbone.

He continued to try to talk in the dark of the attack. But Jacopo was always hasty, and after these years his breath was bad. The time came, he let himself flounder forward into Jacopo's arms, nightcoat dragging, and then Jacopo pushed him away. In the moment of consequence like the bending of a saw blade, he remembered a work of intimate draftsmanship, a harem of classical nudes packed together white and featureless like eels. There in the dark, white, featureless except for sexual distinctions, posing uncomfortable, abundant, in the airless dark. One model sat for all, he saw their cluster of similarities, the white details repeated over and over, and as he let go and fell he saw them the more clearly. He wondered, touching the cold of the etching, who might disturb the prohibitive blacks and grays of their tiring watch behind the faintly Egyptian door.

He fell and rolled over, squashing in his pocket a piece of Romano cheese.

Waiting, afraid to move, Adeppi stared at the spot where Edouard lay. He heard footsteps climbing from the weeded canal and another who watched, rattling his equipment, wet, stole to the victim. Fumbling hands poised over the fallen head, a cautious look. Satisfied with the loneliness, the black figure stooped and, catching hold of the shoulders, dragged the body under the quai.

Jacopo ran, the coat flew off his back. When he was out of sight, his relief echoed down in laughter. And Adeppi smelled the top waters of a farther canal, heard the swimming of sated rats. From up there came the sudden "sciar" of colliding boatmen.

Interview with the Alpini

Several miles from the Gatto and a few hours before morning, Nino finally quit the jurisdiction of this city. Boarding a small gauge train of three cars, he found himself after a time pulling up a low range of mountains from the ridges of which he could see the ocean, a bird-breast blue, flat, in the morning haze flitting with Venetian sails. The black cock's feather curled like a sickle from his Swiss cap, the helmet at his side was filled with grapes. He tapped his cleated boots on a muddy carpet, hugging about him his rifle, pick, and canisters, and watched for signs of the next village. One other in the compartment seemed also not to have slept that night.

The priest Dolce looked at Nino with eyes that retreated on either side of the white bridge of the nose into embittered catacombs and which, now sharp for the truth, now soft as dusk, held the beholder's glance as if, in a moment, they would divulge some bit of personal unfortunate news.

Dolce slipped the cross into the folds of his gown and, suddenly fastidious, lifted his arms and ran the fingers of both hands delicately along the edges of his thin hat, smoothing the brim. He looked out of the window, straight of spine, folding his hands in his lap. As he did so, the three segments of the train struck a curve in the Apennine tracks, glass rattled, chandeliers smashed bottom up against the roof of the cars. Dolce fell in a corner and a sharp tooth came through his lip. There was a trembling in the string that tied the thin hat to his collar. The whistling stopped, and from where they sat they could hear the stoker laboring his shovel.

Nino's helmet had been upturned and grapes rolled through the compartment, back and forth, as the train sped up the mountain. By the attitude of the priest, half on his side and chin pressed against his breastbone, a slight pulsing at the temples and a harsh, wide expression to the eyes, Nino dared not touch him but took his seat again to wait. He felt that the priest had been speaking all the while.

Nino stood up, holding to the sash.

"Secrets. And I suspect," Dolce's words came cold and accusing, after a moment, "no saint to guard your nights."

Dolce did not move. Then one hand drew from under the robes a handkerchief with which he daubed at the puncture on his mouth. He watched Nino persistently, wiped the wound, stared and half smiled as if the soldier had surprised him with a blow. The carriage rolled and the priest with it.

Nino sat down, pushing the tassels away from his knee. He whispered, "I'll tell you, Padre. The secret. It was a bad night." Leaning close his wide mouth and frizzled moustache, "Put away the handkerchief."

Now the priest's head began to jerk toward the speaker, away, near again, and Nino put his hand on the chest of the furtive listener. There was a pounding on the loose glass, and over the turning of the wheels came the sounds of the train master, shaking the handle, screaming at them the obscure name of the approaching town. The sun probed into the priest's corner.

"Adeppi," shouted Nino, "one by the name of Adeppi, Padre, a small boy."

Dolce was up, and before the train could stop, had climbed briskly to the ground. His feet moved rapidly, invisibly; his head was down. As he passed beneath the soldier's window, without looking up, his face hidden under the brim, he lifted his hand curtly—he shielded his gesture with the other sleeve—in the sign of the cross. And he continued on to the station hut, kicking the dust with his little black-pointed boots.

3

...The Ponte Beffa, short of span, high of arch, crowned with flowers and a lady riding on a pillion. Part of its battlement is in decay; it is crossed by many. A troop of eels doze beneath in a pool and their dull electrical tails disengage, then sink in the mud. Adeppi gives them a kick with his toes. The edges of his trousers have un-raveled in the summer and his belt become tight. His mouth is dirty, in seclusion he has been sunning him-self on a rock and sleeping under the bridge, preferring the Ponte Beffa to the Gatto.

But now he hears the sound of wandering feet and watches the head bobbing just visible above the curve of the stony half-moon. The accordionist trudges up over the canal and stuffs the last of his cigarette under the lady's pillion. He is unshaved. Each day he has crossed at the same time, followed by no children or rats, approaching from the west one day, the east the next. On top of the bridge he opens a knapsack, then continues. Jacopo's earrings flash in the sun. He dares not speak to the young girls waiting their turn at the bridge.

Directly overhead, the sounds caught in the city's draining cavern, Adeppi hears suddenly that the accordionist is playing a reedy tune to walk by, faintly, with one hand. The hand goes over the keys as a man absently fingers a few coins in his pocket. Adeppi shuts his mouth firmly, looks away, down at his shadow curled into a ball at his feet. "O Sole Mio"—but even this cannot make him hail his friend.

He disappears.

The bakery walls continued hour on hour their bluish molding, and the boy listened for the emerging of mice. Now and then from under the window Adeppi heard the slapping of sandals as pairs of young men passed, or the irregular, indifferent gait of a limping soldier. Beyond the city came the soft thousand murmur of troops in transit, quartered on the ground, asleep in the fields. On his breath was the smell of anchovy. The boy's knees were drawn up as he settled himself. One of the small, formless hands hung over the side of the bed, swinging back and forth, reaching for the tops of boots or whatever crouched coiled under the ropes stretched for springs.

"Edouard," he whispered, "wake up, Edouard. Bondi, Edouard, bondi! Do you wink at me, old man? Wake up there!"

Without lifting his head from the pillow, Adeppi turned sharply, restlessly, in the opposite direction, his other cheek to the musty cloth. The chest and knees were kept rigid, their stiffness for the appearance of sleep. His eyes were large in the darkness. An empty market smell of mortar and carter's grease, wicker, and warm geraniums came from the city moored so long on the hillside. Below them, the madonna lay buried in her case and, further down, the femurs of entombed monks grew chilled. Summer prowled the unnumbered doorways. Adeppi smelled the greenness of a few vats of wine and the scent of thieves now rousing themselves with basins of cold water. He began to scratch his scalp. Far away he heard the bending of the gondoliers at their midnight task, calling passengers.

Suddenly there was a noise in the street, a lone figure on his nightly way came into an unidentified square across which drifted the smell of sack-stuffed mattresses and the hissing of a small fire extinguishing itself on the open, watery floor of the gabinetto. Adeppi heard him pause, swing around, and fall up short against the door, weakly, with expelled breath. He could feel him look up unsteadily at the trussed window and steep roof, searching after the burning chestnut. With a rope, he would hoist himself to the balcony, a kick at the shutter, and then death for Edouard, too ill to stir.

More steps, the man stumbled in the darkness. There was no dog to drive him off, chase him who had with new energy ventured upon the streets. Adeppi got out of bed and crouched at the foot. An accordion struck up like a gramophone deep in the tombs and cellars. Then the boy, taking a breath and shaking his fist at the shutter, "Via!" he dared call weakly in his high voice, "Via!"

The music stopped short. None such had been heard since the closing of the Gatto, no such frightening sound as that of music moving across the barricaded off-quarters of a silent city, across the back houses, gardens, and chimneys. The boy flung out the shutters, crept onto the balcony and, lifting himself, leaned over. "Via, via!" he whispered softly again but did not move. He was not agile, he trembled in the chill, the short low forehead stared down from the balustrade at the bellows of the accordion, the invisible fingers on the keys. Jacopo stepped forward and held out his hands until Adeppi, who finally climbed to a seat on the ledge, dumbly pressed his palms to his chest and jumped into the outstretched arms.

Two carabinieri emerged from around the corner at a trot and, running close together, shoulder to shoulder, gesticulating for silence, they approached and stood fanning themselves with leathern, cockaded hats. The accordion sagged.

"Buona sera," said one of the carabinieri and nudged his companion. They were short with heavy brows and tight black eyes and on the forehead of each was impressed the red markings of a Napoleonic hat. Their tunics were stained with the oil of canned fish. They winked at each other, swinging the rifles.

"Over here, please," ordered the carabinieri and re-

treated. Jacopo walked with bent knees, the fingers tat-
tooing against his thighs, thin, looking over his shoulder toward the accordion. The carabinieri closed upon
him, one reached out and touched the earrings.

"I am too young, Caporale, and sick. Someone else,
per favore…" Jacopo pulled the coat up on each shoulder, half fallen forward, rested against the wall. The
carabinieri stood but a hand's pace in front. Jacopo
paused. Beaten back against the tiles, eyes averted, he
whistled quickly between his teeth. "The winter," he
added, "I would die in it."

The men threw back their heads, laughing, bent down
to lay their rifles in the street. Their hands reached out
together, a muscled arm, a graceful gesture, stumbling
in the shadow, and one of the pendants was torn from
Jacopo's ear. The soldier dropped it into his trousers.

"Once more, Caporale, don't touch me." Softly, speaking to the ground: "The child would not see me go."

The prickly beards close together, they turned so that
the flat stripes on their trousers twisted in the moonlight. "He must look the other way then."

Jacopo covered himself from the weight of their tufted
sleeves. "Infermo," he cried as they herded him, kicking
with their boots, "infermo!" Dropping his arms, Jacopo
attempted to slip past the carabinieri with breaths of
white tobacco and the sweet stewed meat of cats captured about the prison. Suddenly they freed him.

"He cannot serve," admitted the first.

"Fievole. Enough." The second nodded and straightened his uniform.

The carabinieri stared with curiosity into Jacopo's face. They picked up his coat.

"No harm, Signore?"

They gestured with open palms, shifting about. They clawed apologetically at the fleas in the sweatbands of their hats. A street dog crept to them, beating its tail, and licked one of the white ankles.

"Your dog, Signore?" Drawing away his foot, "He has a cold tongue." They laughed, showing the spaces between their teeth.

"I am Guiglielmo," said the first.

"And I Gregario Fabbisogno," mumbled the other.

Jacopo was silent.

They coughed, took up their rifles inconspicuously, and hurried away.

Three crude women were scratched in charcoal on the stones of the first portion of the aqueduct and under the drawing in childish script were the words, "Salve, Salve, Salve." In the night a wolf or dog had rubbed his quarters against the Roman watercourse and blurred this sign and its inscription which was written low near the ground. The broken butts of the aqueduct, like sepulchres, were visible across the olive hills; from them came the sound of falling pebbles and the sound of rats walking the tunnel on their long way to Rome.

In the valley a band of figures, stepping on the ties of the small gauge railroad track, returned from saluting the statuette of the madonna at the Bocca di Piazza. The men carried their coats over their arms.

"Let them pass," said Jacopo and they huddled forward together, trailed by a cowed dog with a basket in its teeth. They dropped from sight behind an embankment, shielding the flames of their candles.

When the valley appeared empty, Jacopo and the boy hurried down the hill, skirting a windowless farm behind which, on a rope, a khaki blanket hung in the sun. Someone shouted at them from the blackness inside the hut, but they ran on. The tracks across the lowland turf were clear, the bare rails which attracted stragglers twisted on their thin bed of coals in the ravine and high on the other side collided with the whorls and fragments of the aqueduct. Lichen crept along the rails, racing the iron. Wind had blown the light ash to the right and left of the tracks and here grew newly scattered yellow flowers.

"Jacopo, where is the train? Have they put down a new road for it?"

They walked forward through the country of solitary animal pens and refuse fallen from brake boxes; straw and oil baked under an expanding sun that turned in the heavens like a boar on its back. Presently they reached a crossing and on this spot, stooping, with his rifle across his shoulder, they met a lonely guard. In daylight Gregario Fabbisogno stood even smaller, his bones were of medieval armor. He looked about hurriedly, as if for his companion the Caporale, and jerked off his tri-cornered hat—with this gesture the mussed black hair fell almost to his back—and bowed. The carabiniere laughed. His toes came through the boots.

"You will have to halt," he declared. And then, seeing Jacopo's earring, "Concittadino!" he exclaimed and patted his shirt front.

Jacopo walked stiffly around the soldier, clucking and nodding his head. He stopped behind him, and the carabiniere wiggled his baggy uniform, not daring to turn. "Your stomach hangs low, compatriot. But your eye is good, it remembers. Fabbisogno? That's right, I remember, too." And Jacopo, with the edge of his hand, struck the back of the policeman's neck.

Slowly the carabiniere got to his feet, disturbing the dust, and kept his eyes on his empty hands which caught the trickling from his nose. The cocked hat lay bottom up by the tracks. He spoke into his hands, "I am on duty."

Jacopo made no move to take back the stolen earring. He looked closely at the carabiniere's unbuttoned uniform. Lightly, carefully, he put his shoe on the man's toes, and from tight lips: "A question, Fabbisogno. When does the train pass? The child would like to see the train."

Gregario Fabbisogno shrugged. He put a finger over his mouth, then pointed to a small enameled medal on his breast. He looked up at the sky and flexed his baggy arms as if he wanted only to be left alone and to stand slouched at attention.

"An answer," said Jacopo, "quick."

And the other, guardedly: "There are days when it does not appear at all. Have you been told it will pass today?"

"I don't ask for myself," Jacopo gently pushed him, "but for the boy."

The carabiniere shook his head. "No train today, bring the child some other time. If it was expected, I'd put that bar down on the crossing. You see I don't."

The sun rolled over them. Under a single stunted cypress leaned a black and white sentry box, upended like a coffin, and inside, heavily shawled and hiding her face, stood Fabbisogno's mother who had carried his lunch from the village. Adeppi ran to her.

"Old woman," he shouted, "when does the train arrive? Will we see it soon?"

She made no movement but to shuffle her feet and draw the shawl closer over her face.

"When will it whistle, woman?" Adeppi struck the wood, peered into the little station, the floor of which was covered with rocks and particles of travel. "Come out. We will look the other way."

"Infermo, infermo," was the faint answer as she clutched at her shawl.

"She is old," said the carabiniere, hanging his head.

Fabbisogno's mother, struggling, turned her back to the door and bruised her hands, feeling for the latch, in her attempt to escape through the rear wall.

The train burst into view a kilometer down the track, and every moment or two its whistle reached high in the air while smoke gathered slowly above the insect engine. Pieces of black tin were bolted to the cars, with funereal caution it approached, looking for obstacles or secreted explosives wedged in the tracks. Fabbisogno ran for his road block, picked up his hat. Jacopo took hold of his collar.

"Signore," begged Fabbisogno, twisting his eyes wide, "Signore, I guard the road!"

The first car, the second, then the third rolled past, the couplings asway like shackles, the passengers sitting straight beside produce and damp munitions. The fireman waved a blistered hand.

"Signal ahead," he shouted. "Water, we must have water at Monte Motteggio."

Jacopo, Adeppi, and the carabiniere pressed as close as they could to the rushing of the wind, the sparks, and smelled the travelers' cold bottles of rosolio.

The train goes out of the valley and once again the afternoon is becalmed, settles moodily to foot. The sky, colored blue as the inside of a shell, is cleaved by a hairline from the distant, lofty, and several heads of the aqueduct so that between them appears an immeasurably thin glimmer of the after-heavens, the clear vacuity beyond the orb. There is no one caught out of the farmyards. It is country without the activity of shoot or sprout, without shadow.

The vendors continue to hawk china molded on the thumbs of Michelangelo over the mountain where the renaissance has failed. But the tartars smuggling from coastal port to port are away and here only an abandoned sundial passes the hours. Two harpies flap uneasily to a haymound, peer about the rose-covered fortifications of the valley, the catholic slopes, the wind shaking their wings, the sun their beaks.

The accordionist and boy leave the carabiniere rubbing his mother's hands with his scratchy claws and turn in circles on the white path, shading their eyes against the glare. Once more Adeppi trails. As he walks, the water rolls in his stomach.

"Who are we going to see now, Jacopo?" he calls and thinks of all who might meet them on the blue floor of the valley. He chews his fingers, looking out for a new face descended from the Longobardi. Adeppi expects every traveler to know him. He waits to be recognized, holds his hands over his head against the sun and is disappointed.

4

La Casa della Contessa, with orange out-buildings, a recent grave which the Contessa would not admit lay on her estate, and an empty aviary, belonged to the old lady and was her fortune.

The Contessa stayed in her room but was remembered by her woman, Arsella, as sitting before the fireplace for an hour each of those days past, wearing a wide green Florentine hat of velvet, face white with the cares of a doge. In that room a diplomat, hurried to the south and a little distance inland from the sea, had been shot before the empty blackened fireplace. The Contessa now kept in her unheated chamber the discovery, which she upturned in cards, that his soul and a wisp of his waistcoat stopped the flue.

Behind the villa, on the ground floor of a small building in which lived Arsella, her mother, and Pipistrello, was a cow of slatternly gray hide. The earth was her pedestal. Her horns were hollow. She had turned gray wading across the fields and now lay with back caved as if under blocks of stone, two delicate forelegs doubled beneath her breast in the straw. Several small chests, covered with dung, were stacked around her. Her whole face was swelled about the tongue which grew large, as did her haunches, while she guarded the stucco and statuary of a milkless past. There was a stain on her side where a liter of red wine had been spilled.

Arsella herself had the bare corroded legs of the cow, thin, white, mature as if she had borne children, and feet that belonged to the field. Year in and out the flannelette skirt was open to the winds that caught her above the knees, a skirt which in its weave had become part of the countryside along with the legs that rubbed against the animal in its dirt. A rosary was gathered at her waist.

Her husband, Pipistrello, was blind; at his wheel, he listened for the shape of the pottery that he turned. Arsella's mother sat beside Pipistrello, and from sunrise to night, held her ears as his clay grated the wood like sandstone. All day, with lips drawn back, she imitated the noise of the wheel, cursing as it ground against the hours. These two, the eyes of Italy, sat to the cow's rear on the other side of the wall, their hair blowing in the heat, waiting for news of the Contessa's death.

Arsella's mother led Pipistrello to his wife's room each night. Then, through the darkness, the old woman would go to her own bed and in the chill, undress. That night

Arsella seated Adeppi on the floor of her mother's room. The old woman removed her short jacket, her narrow skirts, until she stood in nothing but a sleeveless hair shirt, old and worn, a thin brown penitent garb that clung to her body. And Arsella's mother looked down at it on her chest and, before kneeling upon her bed, pulled it aside and scratched. Long ago it had been stitched unevenly up the front and little punishment remained in it. She had come upon it thinking the hair belonged to the disciples. In winter it broke the wind.

"Why do you wear that coat?" asked Adeppi. He sat against the wall with his legs straight on the floor and stared at the mouseback when she caught the light of the moon. He heard Arsella and Pipistrello fluttering in their half of the building.

"Protect me!" cried the old woman, "Protect me!" She put her hands over her breast. "Arsella, he questions me!" She tapped on the wall, but there was no answer. She pulled at the shirt and burrowed into the bed.

"Are you going to leave me here? Madre, the animals!"

Adeppi got up and looked out of the window upon rows of knotted, miniature tree growths that disappeared silently with their misty branches into the darkness. The hair shirt smelled like ash, the old woman fretting her sorry horsehair, the same who had chased him, shaking her underskirts, screaming, "Signorina, Signorina," spitting and descending the crooked streetways.

Arsella's mother had had sons illiterate as she. One in his youth had fled with a green-complexioned actor not to return; another died at birth; one more was stabbed upon a rock after a far swim in the Adriatic— the old woman barren now of recruits for either wolves or lambs, flat on her back with only her daughter, a simonist, near should she be picked again for castigation by the powers of night.

Outside a whelp began to bay, a political signal for inbred dogs and hungry factions. Its voice was dry, almost a squeal. "Concittadino," it faintly howled to the small boy, "Coraggio! "

Adeppi took hold of the old woman's water pitcher, put it to his lips and began to spit like a Tuscan fountain. He lay down under a stick from which spaghetti hung in white threads.

Adeppi's Dream

Nino on a windy corner. Behind him a wolf, with pups still dragging at the dugs, laps the rain. A long indistinct coat falls from his throat to boots. For a moment his face contorts as if, come purposely back to a distant village, he sees what he is looking for.

Nino, the fatherless. Escaped, only to take up this post begrudgingly. At times the wind pushes him around the corner, but he reappears. He pulls at the bottom of his coat, bares one knee and a round of bandage. He glances up, then proudly points at the wound, brushing stupidly the black hair from his eyes. He cups his hands, he is calling into the darkness, the Italian autumn, the hoarse whisper through the storm in the city.

"It will not heal! It will not heal, fratello mio...."

He is lost in the formlessness of the unruly coat, he forces the guitar inside again. "Bene," he mutters and nods his head. The black stones ring lightly, as a goat walking its quick pace. The narrowness and irregularity of the masonry of sixteen arches bitten by the teeth of centuries close above, the shuttered façades of private house or bordello offer no entrance, pooling their rain in a common spring into which he steps to the ankles.

Nino limps aggressively, walking on the strength of his wounds which in his country are congenital; he stops at every off-shooting passageway, his face close to the walls, musette bag at rest by his feet, and reaches his hand against the wet stones, peers, attempting to find a street name painted there: *Via Tozzo, Via Saccheggio, Via Santa Maria della Salute.* He is baffled by what he reads.

At every corner it is the same, the piazza is gone, as if some trenchant martyr has lifted a stone to the hole. Shut in with the rain. Nino lowers his head, moves rapidly, darkened with the Mediterranean tan that will never fade. It is like Nino to take shelter, expecting death.

Nino leans down, his lips begin to rise and deflate. The bag in one hand, the pistol in the other, he stoops further and thrusts his face along the muzzle. Then: "Peccatore, tell Edouard 'Nino sends his love!'"

He shoots.

At dawn Arsella found Adeppi sleeping between the cow's front legs. Sunlight brightened the yellow of the horns. He lay on the first morning, sore and innocent of the manner in which he as the child and the cow as the Bible's mistaken sheep mocked the nativity of the creche, asleep on the thin and sacred straw which Arsella herself had pitched to the animal.

She stepped outside, and as the sun wrinkled the skirt across her buttocks, began drawing her long hair into a bun.

"Get up, get up, Pipistrello," shouted the old woman above.

Pinned to the back of Arsella's door and the only decoration in the room was a bleeding heart with brambles, printed on a piece of curled parchment the size of a playing card. The arteries, cut close, were painted flamboyantly and crowned with gilt; the thorns, a mustard green, went deep. Each morning Arsella put her lips to it. Pipistrello kissed nothing and wore a medallion down his spine instead; nevertheless, he kept something for himself in the darkness.

Arsella's was a room in which a blind man and his wife might well sleep. It was narrow, and except for the bed, empty like a cubicle kept over the years for hire with a cold floor and a price on the space in which two might lie side by side. At the corners were four rude beams, in the sunlight caught afire, and only the wood, bronze as the planking in a stable, marked the room as distinct from any to be found in the lower courses of Rome, stripped bare and convenient, awaiting occupation. The hand-illuminated heart hung from its nail in place of coat hook or calendar. It could be seen only if the door was closed—this part of the body hung like a lung extricated from its mass—and so bared, displayed the frightening inaccuracies of the imagination. Adeppi with his first glance learned that thorns grow inside the chest.

"Perchè, Arsella, perchè?" and added, "I don't believe it."

"God the Father," she answered from the bed, "anything is possible."

Arsella was born in a vineyard, was found to be a girl by an old man nearby and was carried in her mother's arms—a throng met them in the village—to the steps of the church, not inside. Her teeth grew cutting upon bits of bread wet in wine. Her flesh was brown and the heels heavy; she grew sanguine quickly and with hardly a trace of the dark madonna about the eyes. She married Pipistrello near the spot where the poet was burned on the windy shore. The ceremony took but a short time, was followed by feasting.

Thereafter Arsella stayed as much as possible in her room at La Casa della Contessa. Pipistrello kept below with his wheel, glazing away endlessly his vessels, the crooked spouts and bowls. From late morning through the afternoon to evening Arsella stretched flat on her stomach, sometimes in sunlight that came through a window at the head of the bed, day air into a monastic cell. She did not pray, lying as the monks could not. There was a twitching in the flank which she did not feel and with head bent there came over the room the sound of immodest breathing.

"Arsella, did he eat the brambles?"

Red, white, and gold, the heart looked full, a crimson mussel without foot or face. Adeppi watched; his eyes were small, close set, the gum in the front of his mouth was bare, his fingers clasped the bed irons. Then he shrugged and turned away.

"Turn him out, Arsella!" shouted the old woman from below, picking at the blinded Pipistrello.

Arsella kept several sacks under the bed. As the days passed, Adeppi drove his hands into the hard weave and grasped what appeared to be the arms and legs of dolls. And he spent days seated on Arsella's mattress in which the woman hid her stomach and chin. His only chore came at dusk when it was his turn to empty the cow's water, dragging it outside in a great tub, wide-rimmed, full as sponge.

Arsella, her eyes close to the mattress, stared through the open window. Adeppi too, with mouth hung open, looked impassively at the cropped earth and hemlock beset by parasites. They smelled the old men burning hay. And as Arsella and Adeppi roosted in the upper story, basking under a sun which made the roof creak, he passed his hand over her shoulder, down the back, sometimes still near the pit of her spine, until it lighted upon her buttocks, beginning to turn and wheel with the humming of the sun and dust high as her hip and low as the falling off of the flesh.

On a late afternoon Arsella pulled one of the long-necked sacks from under the bed and slipped away. She and Adeppi, the bag between them, blinked again in the sunlight. Pipistrello leaned near, smoking a cigarette. He lifted his face to tell the time of the sun.

"Arsella, un momento..." Pipistrello mysteriously waved the bit of cigarette, came toward them. His brow was severe with an effort to open the round lids. "Un momento," he ordered. He wore a leather jacket gathered close to the waist and on the arm a black band. There were flecks of feather and pollen in his hair, the hands were stiff and horned from his potter's work. On his feet he wore only a pair of light stockings. In the noonday sun he caught Arsella's shoulder and roughly, his fingers strong, felt her face, chest, and behind her ears under the hair, at arm's length the brusque exercise by which he knew her. Silently Adeppi took the sack.

She eluded him, and Pipistrello did not attempt to follow, turning after them abruptly and standing still, his skull so tilted and the chin lifted that, had he been able to see, he would have been staring over their heads and into the olive clouds. He brushed at the shadow under his eyes.

"Prudenza," he called while she could still hear. "Prudenza."

Arsella went first down the path. It was rocky and a white distance to the nearest shade. The neck of her shirt was cut as low in back as in the front. There, and at her knees, Adeppi could see the white line of her single undergarment. They passed stakes to which animals were no longer tethered. Now and then they crossed over reddish barricades of barbed wire by climbing on stones that had been heaped to serve as stiles. Arsella walked as if she were pushing a great load; her toes were black.

At the bottom of the hill sat an old man. He smoked a scalding hooked clay pipe which glowed brightly up to the stained reed of the stem. He had removed his shirt and draped it over his head as a sun hat. His arms rested on his knees and almost entirely hid the chest skewered with age. A goose with a broken neck lay against his foot.

"Arsella, wait. That man, there, the man who eats brambles!"

"Can't you see," she answered, "he has a goose to eat."

Before they could continue, the old man dropped his pipe, caught up the bird, and hugged it to his chest like a thin dog clawing a moth. The pipe lay smoldering in the grass. The goose's body—it was enemy to rodents and the pups of wolves—smeared blood from the old man's foreflank to his collarbone.

"Via, via!" he shouted as loud as he could.

They passed. There were a few farms and the dung heaps contained great holes, gouged nightly by wily jaws. The earth looked as it did the first day it worked itself up from the sea. Not a laugh rang out across a country still deep in its half-century siesta.

Arsella's sack was light, yet now and then she let it drag behind her feet on the loose path. Once she stopped, took off her rosary, and gave it to the boy.

They reached the hut at the same moment a priest approached from the opposite direction, down the hillside, beating his skirts. He was breathless and fanned himself with his black hat. His cassock was wrinkled, having been drawn close these nights against the chill.

"The village, Signora," he inquired and flapped the dust. "South, my child, or north?"

He did not look at Adeppi. Arsella pointed and Dolce sped away, swerving further from the forked meeting place of the hut.

Adeppi recognized the hut, the same from which he and Jacopo had been hailed on the day they hunted for the villa. Up one side reaching from the debris to the roof top was the pale imprint of a twice life-size cross, all that remained of the crucifix which, like a damaged chimney, had been torn down. The hut was small but it contained eight rooms, two by two, one pair behind the next. There was neither a door in the doorway nor glass in the windows. In the first room a small child, yellow-skinned, knelt upon a narrow bench with its peaked face forward over a tin saucer of wine.

"Brother Bolo," called Arsella.

The child glanced about, unable to run, then drew its body down even tighter to the bench. After a moment it dipped one of its hands into the wine and began, squinting its eyes at Arsella, to lick the fingers and palm. They did not enter. The next pair of rooms were empty but around the walls were hung a few alms cups. The floor was brown and yellow, the tile tracked with dirt and a fine sifting of trampled pottery and veneer. In the third pair the fresh ashes of a fire lay beaten in a corner. There was a cold current in these shadows that could rot the hardwood; the breech of a small rusted weapon sat on its tripod under the window in a draft of sunlight. In the last pair they found him. Bolo filled the left-hand room, bounded by the sides, top, and bottom of his cell, all parts of him swelled to the partitions buried within the hills and canal-cut plains of the dark country that did not comb its hair. He wore a coat with high buckled collar, close together and prominently he carried his small hands, which, tapering of finger, were clean and soft to the touch. On his left hand was the sacred seal.

"I return your greeting," said Brother Bolo quickly and reached for the sack. Arsella handed it to him, pinched Adeppi's arm.

Bolo untied the strings. He felt to the bottom and then by a wing drew forth a cherubim that had flown over the heads of the Volto Santos in the hour of prayer.

"Oh, holy, true, and golden cross, which was adorned with his body and watered with his sweet tears, by thy healing virtue and thy power, defend my body from mischance, and by thy good pleasure, let me make a good confession when I die." Brother Bolo took a breath. Carefully he laid the cherubim on the table. He leaned forward and blew the road dust from it.

"If you ever get to St. Peter's, Pipistrello's wife, you shall see him, safely hanging again from his wire. But at a price." The cherubim's knees were drawn up so that he might run in the air. "If you look closely you'll know him at the hour of vespers. Notice the broken wing, Pipistrello's wife."

"It's nothing, Bolo," she answered.

"Fifty lire for that wing. To be deducted." He put his fingers under its arms and lifted. Bolo hung his sharp eyes sleepily and began to pick at the gilt with a fingernail. From the hut's first rooms came the sound of the child humming a wordless song.

"Adeppi, shall we part with the little angel?"

"Yes." But he was listening to the child's wandering voice.

Away from the beatific font and in Bolo's grasp the cherubim weighed less than a kilo.

"How much for it?"

"Your pleasure, Brother Bolo."

"It will pass through other hands than mine before Rome sees it again; and if it is ground for mortar before then, well, it will bring little...."

"Bolo, each is a dove...."

"The golden holocaust, Pipistrello's wife. Each is a bead that has been cast off in prayer."

"Signore," Adeppi interrupted and flung off Arsella's hand, "I know where there is a madonna, in the Bocca di Piazza, a madonna, Signore!" And reaching up, he gestured, once more exclaimed, "Madonna!", urged Bolo to follow and struck the good wing so that the cherubim fell loose and broke on the floor.

"O sacrilegio, sacrilegio," cried Arsella softly and drew back from the pieces.

It is dusk when Gregario Fabbisogno comes upon the edge of the hillock and crouches with his rifle at port arms, fearful and with noisy ear, having deserted his post to the owls. His beard has grown in the last hour, he must make a place for himself in the grass. Is it not too late to discover the trench ringed with bloody sticks? No one will take him in tonight. He has not been commissioned to build a fire. Below, his mother is mad at the crossing. Fabbisogno's trousers balloon; he remembers they have been called his face and spits through his wide teeth. He protects himself with the gun as the dew comes and he sees the shadows of foes gathering behind the hut. He keeps pulling his mouth awry and listening for the tread of donkeys loaded with cannon and packs instead of bells. It is a night to challenge skeletons bound upright to the tops of haystacks or to kill the geese dancing upon the graves.

Fabbisogno takes his stand before the hut.

"What is moving there!"

The cold of the earth passes into his boots and he looks within a hundred paces of the outpost of sated crows. Exclaiming, "I am on duty!" he shoots at the shadowy figure, starts as the bullet imbeds itself in the chimney stone. Brother Bolo clasps his hands and falls; the child carries him a cup of wine.

Gregario Fabbisogno runs, with a frown that by its ignorance and solemnity covers his desire to shoot again, dark as the moon against which he leans for breath.

5

Christ had a sharp face. Dolce knew every line of it. All the quixotic notions of suffering and the guard-watched severity with which that heavy head lay to its side were bounded in limitless compensation as dignity upon a few beams.

Down the length of the vinegar peninsula, in a country that made much of the birth and worshipped more the bearer, Dolce was peculiar for his transfixion upon him who, a man and by a mob of men, was crucified on the ground and hoisted into the air. If he had walked in this village on this evening his face would have worn a further and befitting sign of a black patch across his eyes. As it was, wearing only benevolent stains, he was remembered by his nervous priest Dolce to be pitiful in awe-striking thoughts of windy illumination. Dolce's passion was known to the Brotherhood as devotion for the face itself and the agony contained in the brown eyes. Dolce carried this exact expression where he went, showing to strangers only his own insignificant suspicion, a trembling chin, meanly concealing the images of wind-beating locks and thorns.

Thus Dolce arrived. After a hard trip he appeared in the city some kilometers below La Casa della Contessa and went directly to the fountain. An old woman ladled him a cup of water. He drank, wiped the dust from his face, and blessed her. He noticed the woman—she lowered her head three or four times backing away—with the same eye that caught the birds at that moment hurrying to roost. Around the square they dropped to the open galleries, following one on the other under the narrow and florid arches darkening to the public spectacle. The old woman hurried behind him and he sat to rest, unaccosted, on the fountain's damp rim. He vigorously proportioned out the city, leveling it so that he might search it, piercing the uniformity of its dusty guise.

He appeared and sat in the Bocca di Piazza well after its hour of crowds. Two hundred feet ahead, his eye in passing found the small shadow-swept resting place of the miniature madonna, posted on the wall like a bird box, and at this distance he recognized her, made the sign. But his attention went to the combs and footways that climbed inward from the false opening of the square, conceived to belie the narrowness beyond, in which those who knew each other might move closely to their purpose. The last bird rose as Dolce snapped his hands at it, winged painfully toward a ledge, veered and fell safely behind a rooftop. All the noise from the inner caves of the city fell short of the square.

The old woman had left her cup and he drank again. He saw on the bottom, glittering under the last sipful of water, a few begged soldi, and he dropped it. He was warned. But he did not leave the sound of the water's continuing splash in its public font. Until he could sit no longer.

Chin jutting in subordinate holy profile, he moved now upon the city that could escape no further, caught intrenched at the end of its own tunnel. He took his steps carefully, not to miss any of the snares spread for him. At dusk, trailing his blackness, he freely exited from the placid, unfamiliar piazza and stole into the avenues of burros bunted with the stretched and rigid shapes of vegetables long hung by twine from the walls, toes inward. The bridge where the stony blue lady sat her pillion was hardly noticeable, the span shallow and the arch slight, squeezed between great sidings of the slaughterhouse. A single woman, without word or excitement, turned her body and face to the wall until he passed.

Dolce pulled sharply at his black brim, tipping it in dismissal. He felt the throat-pinching emotions of the stranger with his scant foreign baggage and dusty britches who, not knowing the way, may thrust himself into good quarters or bed and on this first night see with an immunity not completely sure against false steps and falls. That sense of being loose in a city similar to the one left, but without memory, offering itself or resisting investigation—its short chambers, kitchens, and roof touching roof—all before morning. About him were the secular playgrounds of the boys, the shrewd originations of young men and their entertainments, and old men. To be strange in such a place, it stirred God's cleric in excitement; he stopped to count the beads.

He continued until he found the unobtrusive entrance to a small church and its dismal surrounding silence. Here he could pause. He stepped cautiously into the center of the narrow street to peer at a small tangle of iron on top—the winds had whirled it—a cross which lay high like the skeleton of a nest fled by the rooks. Dolce admired it, a sudden prayer for the magnanimous brown eyes, at death raised and looking through the breasts of the stoners to clouds beyond.

Dolce, without guidance, on a crooked branch of the street and through the darkness, found his way to the Gatto. After walking twice past it, he turned and presented himself at the door, thinking of the pension above for the night. The proprietress did not let him into the caffè but took him around the outside to an opening meant for exit and up the stairs. She climbed quickly and Dolce followed at last and despite fatigue into a hallway above.

Several doors opened a head's width on darkened rooms, and Dolce heard a man, two men mutter; but the proprietress took the placard number from a door as if, numberless, it was his. She went in before him and brushed away an old pair of trousers, swept some coins into her bosom. Her dress was fastened at the shoulder by rosettes and had no sleeves. She stepped aside and Dolce entered; eyes on him, she breathed heavily.

"In the morning, Holy Father," she said, "open the window." She took the light.

He discovered a candle on the bottom of a drawer pried loose from the commode. The image of the woman was before him, her luminous form impressed on the darkness, hands on her slight and transparent hips. Fitting, for Dolce thought of cities as old buildings superintended by women, giving shelter without comfort—as one might be taken into an almshouse—and harboring those from the street merely for the experience of a strange face and strange demands which they could exact themselves to meet with laughter or fear. He wondered what sins the proprietress had assumed for which there was no punishment in this city.

The candle by one heel, Dolce sat on the bed which sagged to the floor and untied his shoes. The room had a narrow air of unoccupancy, the sleepers who had come to it took away with them the soiled linen. Still he smelled an odor not from the wood alone. He put his hat on the pillow next to the gray spot where he would rest his head. Putting the proprietress out of mind, he rose in stockinged feet. He rubbed salt on his teeth and splashed his eyes with water. He gathered up his skirts, leaded about the hems so that each step brought a remindful blow to his ankles, and knelt, one knee then the other falling into place. His hands were white in the clasp. He put his forehead to the wall and began to talk, quite loudly.

He was in the darkest corner and kneeling as low as possible to the floor. If they should burst in upon him suddenly, bringing the curious light over their shoulders, he would not be seen at once nor his privacy violated before he could unclasp his hands and order them away again. He spoke loudly so that they might not think to listen, and the decoying candle, mounted on the farthest wall, burned as if he had just stepped out. It was his habit to so prostrate himself: all the more, since to leave his bent back unprotected to the openness of the room increased his nervousness until he was sick and longed to look around. He feared the sudden shout. And while he talked, he coughed, paused, cleared his throat, the confidence of his voice keeping him rooted and able to contend with the anxieties of a communion which doubled him over like one insensible.

This day he had taken only water. Dolce prayed and confessed on water, a few drops rigidly devoured. The dogs would not drink when he approached, and he went dry if the animals had been at the pond before him with their heads down and muzzles drawing from the still surface by tongue and through nostrils. Dolce was one for the edge of the forest, his clearings were crossed only on the bridge of a shadow, he could not drink without disturbing the water and making the mud rise.

In confession he crouched biting at his master's heels. Dolce did not confess the omissions and grievances of a few hours before—these present reflexes of wickedness went unmentioned until their turn should come after consideration. He concentrated instead upon smashing the most innocent days of earlier years. He saw Christ patiently impaled in a high-backed chair.

At last he went to the bed. He took the hat from the pillow and lay in its place a plain fraternal medallion that had been chained on his girth. He slept, and his hand was raised above the head and cupped defensively as if to catch some weight hurled out of the heavens through the roof.

The Confession

In the novitiate we were cruel. Jesu Christe Saviour. There was an old woman who came every day to the low wall around our monastery and begged for instruction. No other women walked so far. Near dusk she watched as we without hair took exercise in a circle. She carried a tall farming rake which she stood against the wall like a tree split dead and sharp by lightning.

"What had Christ to say for the old woman?

"What comfort for the defenseless?

"Let me walk with you."

These things she shouted, and if none of us raised our heads, she was likely to catch up a handful of dirt and throw it at us novices. But if the little bell rang—it was a soft mournful sound not heard any distance from the monastery—she hobbled off, dragging the rake.

"Chastise me, chastise me, you priests."

I can hear her yet. I did not pity her. Jesu Christe.

She appeared first in winter without a word, and we thought her the mother of one of us, come to beg us back, to claim us from the icy grip of the Order. If there was a last ray of sun, she would lean her elbows on the low stone and begin to nod her head up and down in approval or encouragement. A lone figure, she participated so foolishly and so regularly. When the winds blew in the darkness, she was there listening for our monotonous footsteps. On winter mornings the road took her below the monastery, and pulling her rake as a sledge— a tin of frozen milk was her load—she waved at us though none answered. By night she returned with the rake swinging across her shoulders like a great scythe; hardly lifting our eyes, we saw the wood cutting the snow until she dropped it to the ground, an old and brittle foot falling on the ice.

Toward spring she began to cry so that we should hear, and as if this were a sound we novices would understand, thinking the voice of misery our voice, our fate, as a hunter knows his hounds. When the briars beyond the wall divulged a few thin rabbits and new shoots broke beneath the rake, she unwrapped her head. In her youth she had not been beautiful. But we forgot her cries when the showers drove down our heads and filled the bowls sooner than we could eat. Jesu Christe Saviour. Many of us sickened in those months.

Spring came.

"Domine Jesu Christe, sancta cruce tua apud me sis, ut me defendas.

"Domine Jesu Christe, proveneranda cruce tua post me sis, ut me guvernes.

"Domine Jesu Christe, probenedicta cruce tua intra me sis, ut me reficeas," we chanted aloud, no longer chilled and walking through the puddles of a green thaw. And at these words the old woman first began to interrupt our prayers, to talk to us as if we might break our circle and crowd around her like boys, with questions or comfort. Receiving no answer, she took to following the prayers.

"Domine Jesu Christe, Domine Jesu Christe," as she stared at us over the wall, lagging a phrase or two behind. None of the holy fathers ever saw this woman. There was no one to send her away. I remember how, old as she was, it looked as if she might dare to climb in amongst us at any moment, just as she shouted down our evening ritual. What shame, Jesu Christe Saviour.

She was not easy to ignore, having begun at odd fearful times to beat one fist into the other to the rhythm of our walk, the motion of justification, uninterrupted, constant, a movement of backs and without rhythm at all. Our eyes were closed, yet there was no escaping her inspection. She watched us with mouth open, then a frown, then beckoned, and we looked alike to her. We came to know: in the morning she waved from a distance, fenced off from us, by evening she was distrait on our right hand. We recited the prayers less frequently. Consumptive with sin, flesh of the devil, an old woman burning worse than ever though temptation was long done, and the church would not turn around to try her.

Jesu Christe. She provoked us. She came before the monks—for her sight were the leather robes—and exclaimed that she was old and of another sex before their cloister. Deaf she was to our silences, and we took a step with hands outstretched to each other's shoulders.

Heaven forbid, Jesu Christe Saviour, but it was the day of visible ascension before we mustered ourselves to put up with her no longer. We stopped. The brown wheel hardly knew how to cease its turning.

"Woman," our spokesman said, "this is the hour!" and raised his arm upright so that the ragged sleeve fell from the bare bone.

"Grazie, grazie, grazie, grazie…" and she hurried as fast as she could to the gate.

We led her to the stable. Brother Bolo, not I, furnished the pelts. One of us pushed her, undetected in the night. There were no horses in the stalls to whinny an alarm or swing their haunches against the planks. Brother Bolo began pulling his pelts from the beams, in generous handfuls destroying his collection of little hides. They were uncured. He had trapped only in the first months of spring.

Two held her arms. We put the lantern at her feet. She was undressed to the waist by another while we spoke Latin. Our bare toes and heels stamped on the straw that remained. From a high rafter overhead and this late at night—he climbed up there when he was free—one of Bolo's traps rang out. The capture made it fall from the wood, and trap and rodent swung in rotation on the length of cord. We hurried.

"You can see for yourselves, you can see for yourselves," murmured the poor woman.

The first pelts stitched together were held immediately in place covering the dugs. They were lain on with
the fur turned in to the body. We knew the hides would
shrink over the years. Brother Bolo counted as he gave
them up but he held them himself while they were sewn.
The sewing was awkward though the old woman was
not pierced. A great seam grew up the front. We made
much of our work and cut away the pieces that did not
fit, snipped off the tails and claws. The woman was told
that the pelts were being sewn with their heads down.
Our shadows fell backward, tall and sharply gowned on
the rough boards, and she looked at these, calling them
one at a time by the names of the disciples.

Finally but a shoulder remained, and this we covered
quickly. What suits do bodies wear beneath the clothes!
What evil fitters to trim this shirt for her without the
demand of God and the authority of the Order, a few
rat skins pieced together in a stable by one novice fat
and one thin. The poor woman's face grew radiant as if
we had pronounced that henceforward her children's
children would go free of sin. Breathlessly we carried
her beyond the monastery grounds and put her on her
feet.

That night we agreed that more like her should wear
the shirt. Forgive me this thought.

Dolce awoke several times and felt a sore—he was
not tender with it—which had started and begun to pain
his lip since the few hours he had left the fountain. He

must learn better not to eat or drink. He blew out the candle, scraping the wax from his fingers. Each time he awoke, he listened and heard nothing. Tomorrow he would surely fling open the window before mass.

6

It was summer. The sun bleached the tiles to deeper shades of red, the sound of a young girl's voice carried far over the hillocks—with the singing even the grinding of the oxen's shoulder could be heard—before fading. Adeppi lifted his head and listened, though his lips curled. Each day's passing brought a new accumulation of dust white as hair to the vines and leaves, their hemlock color was not seen. Adeppi continued to stroke the woman before the open window. Children run to pat the donkey's haunch or throw their arms around its neck, and he, like the rest, would have clapped after the little animal as it trotted through the grove dropping its new dung. La Casa della Contessa had only its forty-stone cow and the throat of this animal was infected with boils. Adeppi preferred Arsella's room to the stall below. Sometimes without a word she shifted under his hand and then he climbed down and at the window watched for a raven or some other winged boy-fowl to tumble across the blue spacious sky, until he returned to her. Or he went to the door and waited. "Permesso?" and if she did not answer, he was free to descend and take the path into the field and shallow pit. She might shout to him there if he did not hurry.

These days they slept from noon to the hour of vespers, the boy lulled away from the urge toward activity, Arsella's constant position making her head nod. She blew on his eyelids until their hands dropped open and they were asleep. The mouths fell loose, trembling to the breath of the unconscious. Their clothes grew damp. Adeppi would wake sullenly and be sent for water. The sun worked upon them while they slept and tired them. "How old you look, Arsella," he would say when they awoke in the shadow. The face changed hourly. The skin was wrinkled where for a long time the fingers had rested under the cheek. And the boy's forehead also, above the eyes, had thickened and become enlarged with the cells that grew randomly in the course of sleep.

The villa lay atop the conventional terraces of the country. They were littered with the broken chips of Pipistrello's unsuccessful pottery, long ago the planted bulbs had died from these terraces. Here too were buried the discarded pieces of the cherubim. When his sleep was thinned away, it was to the seven artificial levels that Adeppi came, breaking down the rims with a bare foot as he patrolled them.

There were colonies of insects that toiled on or fought

for the terraces: the two-heads, as long as his finger and deep black. If the shells of the jointed body were split, they were found to be hollow and yet able to keep alive even when so ruptured and filled with sand. The living weight of the two-heads was carried outside the shells and to the front in the double appendages. During battle, they fought to tear through the globular mass of these heavily connected lobes. As long as the heads remained together sharing ducts and tissues, there was no need of the body. Though without the shells which carried their legs, they were unable to walk.

Adeppi disturbed the two-heads' natural torment. He held them to the light and they were translucent, some had raveling holes in their black sides, and he strung these together on a twig, on sharp skewers. They were a locust species, transmuted on the grounds of La Casa della Contessa, hordes that had turned against themselves. He sat watching them or lay on his belly watching them, like a cat that has lost part of its senses through a wound in the eye and sitting upright, waits wondering with the other. Sometimes a handful of earth came down and destroyed them, as they were not wormlike and could live only above ground.

Attempting to pass from one terrace to the next, the two-heads killed each other by striking tenaciously at the doubly large target of the face. They lay in the sun, black, dry as kelp. Unlike most insects, a fall from a ledge to a bit of soft earth below could injure them; many were barely able to drag themselves to safe ground and took days to heal. They had forgotten how to denude the olive trees and their afternoons were confined to scaling the terraces, that miniature cleft landscape whose borders were treacherous and stripped of pebbles.

"Look how they crawl, Arsella!" he tried to say, eyes fixed on their efforts which were only to keep themselves marching in the sun. He spent hours on this terrace watching the bugs move in circles that would not keep their order as an old garden sank to decay. He covered his knees with cinders and dug his feet into the low vermin outline of the insects' fortresses. These somber in-between hours he spent surrounded by the creatures of his fourteen hundred days passing and repassing in smoking expeditions. "They have no wings, Arsella." But she did not answer, only put an arm over her eyes.

By sunset Adeppi, Arsella, Pipistrello, all were on their feet, the recumbency of the forenoon was done, and they began to drag over the stones and caked surface of the well yard; in the coolness, working. All three could be seen pulling the cow from its bed, wiping at it with a great quilted rag, picking the parasites from its ear. At last it was beyond the door, twitching its stifled hide to the open air.

"Breathe," Arsella commanded, "breathe!" But it had not the will. So night came to the scraping of the two-tongued fork, the poor dull-witted animal finally guided and beaten into place by the blind man, woman, and boy tugging upon its soft horns.

"A load of wood, Pipistrello. If you please."

Arsella's hair was undone by dusk and it swayed unkempt as she retreated again up the leaning stair, hand across her breast, climbing once more into the unlighted rooms.

It was a night for the hounds to run. Adeppi could hear them fleeting through the baleful mists with bellies and chests compactly forward. Such a hot night for coursing, outdistancing those who followed in ancient velveteen, their epees electrified. No mastiffs these, but the inbred packs whose prey, when run to ground, came to no harm. He felt them circling the villa, giving chase to the great rat tails distended rigidly from the bones of the quarters, damp and never winding, keeping to one exhausting path unless distracted by the far-off horn. The night smelled of the phantoms, what a squealing if one were lost! The gray dogs, in pursuit but not marauding, ran through this summer afterdark; slowed to a sudden trot, they stalked across the empty trysting places, then off again, jowls fastidiously dripping ground meal and bone. Atop the aqueduct they did not lose their footing, scaled like flesh-eating sheep the walls of a monastery, now scolded and called back by the weary whippers of bad spirit emerging from the bog. A lost warning, in the darkness unable to see, man and hound perspiring and snapping expectantly: when women were behind walls and the hand-hammered latch. He heard their blood running fast and cold, their long lines bounding past time-telling statuary and into shrubs that tore their hides. He heard them panting as if there would be rain. The dogs of unrest—those that held their whining and would not stand for chains—were hard by. Ears flat, brains dry, plummeting over stilled fields like birds with wings drawn in, searching—but there was no infant left out of doors. The canescent animals were loose. The prints were fresh in the dew, the low shoots shaken. Woe to them crouched in the rushes; the hound was out.

Adeppi stayed close to the villa. Back and forth he marched, never beyond sight of the prow of the roof beam glistening like a cliff's tooth through the fog bank. He paced his childhood's raided buildings, bareheaded, now and then staring above as if he had never been inside.

He carried the black pot of the mandolin against his chest. Every few minutes he stopped, spread his feet wide, and as best he could swung arm and mandolin upwards and outwards toward the window that had no balcony. He was glad for the mists which drove away the wanderers and left him alone, wishing for loneliness and a land covered with sea-smoke so that he might wake her from below on the tumultuous green and she, from the high familiar room, look down to find him posted, attendant, in the company of sharp stones and the nightly well-plumed owl. *Avanti, avanti.* But he would take good time. He expected that she would listen without smiling, then thrust head and shoulders into the darkness and give her nightdress to the touch of the fog. Only the mandolin would be found by morning beneath the window.

Even the ferns themselves were fending off the dogs with their sting, and he watched to see the yet undiscouraged animals mounting the cloud banks as stone stairs, rats faithfully thronging the mist's deserted incline, ending in fall. Behind them, the men were out, challenging each other as they hurried to their selected trees. All except Pipistrello who was asleep in his black cap.

At last the fog was moving. It too was impatient and rolled high against Arsella's window, then collapsed and fled, every quarter hour torn with hurry. Adeppi looped the mandolin cord twice round his throat. The instrument, weightless, darkly lacquered, swayed as he brushed wet leaves and stumbled, muffling the strings, the fretted neck, until he should allow its music to start with the loudness and desire of three viols.

The first stanza was simply to be sure no jealous ear was listening. A few notes—far apart as if the fingers were too short to strike all the strings at once—and a hasty silence. The next stanza was hummed for his own pleasure. He had decided to kneel, and his head was still bent in case of interruption and a thoughtless, vicious blow. It was in this position, his eyes burning, that he saw the single column of insects winding slowly outward from the terraces, over the dew. One he crushed with his fist and the rest halted. He hit another and the two-heads turned back, blindly leaving him the ground under the window. Again he took the mandolin in his arms.

Now he sang, and this stanza was meant to bring her from the bed. The stringed instrument and his voice, yet soft, sounded foreign amidst the dark, the white, and the earth smelling of undersoil and shallow graves.

"Who is it?" She heard with ears more ready than he expected. But before he could answer, she cried, "Via costà con gli altri cani!" The mist that had been rounding and rounding the house now suddenly darted and disappeared, sucked into the open window past where she hid.

How serious she was. He fell, separating himself from the prickly shadows, and ran midway to the glistening wall, held up the mandolin in both hands.

"Arsella. Do you see me?" He turned sharply, waving the instrument, seeking to part the fog.

Letting the mandolin hang free, he rubbed his fingers, short and wide-spread. In the next silence he heard a sound of bare feet; she had stepped from one side of the window to the other. Never had she listened so closely.

"Perchè mi schiante?"

It was a low bloodless phrase that made his fingers light again on the frets, otherwise he did not move. She had pulled the tongue from the flower. And he saw her. She leaned from the window—so far that he could see the round of her back—and her arms stretched down, pushing the stone, the two ends of her shawl hung down.

"Perchè, Adeppi?"

He bowed, there could be no answer. She had dragged a sheet from the bed and, flung around her, still a corner flapped out of the window. Against it fluttered the dark tails of the shawl. One and the other, they were alone. He knew that at this moment the courtier's horse stood peacefully. He breathed full like a partridge. He sang loudly now, lost in a wood, until he heard Arsella turn suddenly from the window and proudly shout, "Mamma. Hear, Mamma? The monello sings!"

They had a light. There were the three of them squeezed at the opening and swinging the lantern over the gray whorls below. Pipistrello was in the middle, even Pipistrello had been awakened for the enjoyment.

"To the left, husband. Move the flame to the left. I saw him. How small he is!" Arsella reached for the lantern herself. "Hear how he trills!"

"Arsella," whined the old woman, "let us sleep."

He ran. He did not look around to see how those in the cramped gallery fought each other but, as far as the terraces, he heard Arsella's shouting, "Ancora una volta, ancora, ancora…"

The dogs were gone.

Adeppi left the mandolin floating on a shallow pond, and when the sun touched the upended neck, the sight of it startled the waking ganders.

At dawn he crept from under one of the aqueduct's great arches and stared upon a countryside which the sun smothered in false fire. Far below, water evaporated from the roof of Brother Bolo's empty shelter; thistles were laid waste before the field mice stirred. All was saturated—the hut, the vineyard, bird nests long fallen to the ground, the irregular train tracks—and the spongy sun grew as if there had been no night. But it was a sun that tides storm or accident in uncertain, backward latitudes where the first secrets of science are vaulted up with the sacristan's greasy anchovy. In the early morning, Adeppi leaned against the towering silent aqueduct, rubbing his eyes, a small figure at the base of the sculptured and sighing pipeline. In the vicinity of the charcoal drawings, he watched the lower paths for the first woman to appear with hair reaching her waist and make an accustomed toilet in the privacy of a corner of one field. But only a gray lamb with red lips called faintly through a noose which choked and tethered it above the sleeping place of the dead shepherd.

An odor of Brother Bolo's black fire was still on the air, an old and abrasive smell as if all hearth fires, put out by pail, returned freshest in the morning, drifting again from the copper spears of the antiquated kingdom's compass. The fire of old alchemists, kitchen keepers, and monastic stokers turned to ash and from ash to ink which dried on parchments secreted in the trunks of trees, a raised city of life lost over plundered and extinguished valleys. The doges were warming their waxen hands again.

Amidst this stretching sea, quiet, steaming, vacated of leathern carriages and gun carriages—only the sun was on its scaffold—stood but one living and visible on the hillside: Adeppi, blood-filled, indolent, with bones sore from a sleep on the rocks. His heart was beating innocently at the side of the sunburnt neck, there was a darkening on his upper lip. He yawned like a small animal of prey contented a few hours after being whelped, sunning itself helplessly between the paws of its dam.

No one stooped to work the fields, the dry brilliant austerity of the morning was untroubled. He descended. But on the edge of the grove he met Pipistrello emerging hesitantly from between the trees as if he too had spent the night in the open. Adeppi stopped and began to make a clucking sound with his tongue against his teeth, threw a stone far to the left, then took deliberately slow and stealthy steps ominously cracking the twigs. All this while he grimaced, sometimes opened his mouth wide and waved his short fat fingers in front of him. Pipistrello waited without question, standing fatefully as he always did when hoping for some foreign mover to pass him by. Finally Adeppi ran at him so that Pipistrello, keeping his face toward the noise, reached behind him for a support in the nearest slender tree. Adeppi caught his arm, then spoke.

"Were you afraid, Pipistrello? I could not speak, friend, this plum silenced me."

The blind man felt quickly for the boy's other hand.

"It is swallowed already, Pipistrello. Mi dispiace. But we'll find you one before noon. Can't you say good morning?"

Adeppi kept fast hold to the blind man, smiling, winking, staring, for Arsella's curled piece of parchment with its bright hues was pinned crookedly upon the man's breast.

"I will lead."

Adeppi held the blind man's cloth at the elbow where it was loose under the joint, pulled and pushed fitfully as if avoiding the lime pit, a hanging branch, the cowcatcher of an electric tram silent as death. Arsella, or even God's wizened, silver-skinned angel, could not better have marked Pipistrello for the boy. All rituals had been stopped, the earth itself stilled with the light, hot and clear. The blinded walked loosely and severely, having taught himself to put his foot forward quickly. Such could walk off the edge of the earth despite the sun. There was no danger for him, only a day by day tempting of disaster and the door that might not be open.

"No tricks!" Pipistrello suddenly exclaimed and wrenched free. The parchment flapped; he did not notice it.

"There is only a hill ahead, elder. It is empty. It looks safe to me." A timid answer, once more taking the blind by the halter of his arm. And Adeppi did look around him to be sure.

But on top of the hill toiled two small figures hardly visible against the heaven. The hill was steep, straw-colored and smooth, so often baked and picked by cultivation that its altitude of sand seemed held on the incline only under the delicate pressure of the sun. The top receded like the peak of a white tent seen rising in the distance. There was nothing for Adeppi and Pipistrello to stumble against, not a cleft stone or root. Still their progress was slight and they climbed slowly. The hill was wide of front, its shoulders obscured far beyond either edge of the curve. The higher they went the less was their inclination to stop and face back toward the descent. Sometimes Pipistrello slipped and Adeppi faithfully lifted him again.

On the summit where a cart road threaded across the plateau for the passage of a few travelers, the minatory creatures labored with a rude lever and pieces of hempen cable thick as tusks. The men could be seen only by the waving of their wide, brass-like hats. They worked to move a boulder intended to mark a station where journeymen might pause and pray. *A Roma.*

Adeppi shaded his eyes. They up there were raising the dust around the rock. They had discovered the sheep, for a bleating came from beneath a ragged summer coat with which they kept it from the sun.

"Do you hear a lamb crying, Pipistrello?"

Wind blew across the hill's middle steepness. It was a breeze that lengthened the slope in a small country. Man and boy, like a thin kite and its young, struggled to keep their feet as the vaguest movement gave sound to the depths below. When Adeppi lifted his eyes to peer up at the pair twisting the boulder, he trembled with the light sensation of falling backward.

The lever had already ground to bits a few lilies placed at the bed of the rock. The old men did not stop for a moment but continued to assault the stone as if being on the summit filled them with obstinate vigor. It was a monument which, when perfectly positioned, would make the approaching donkey and its rider shy, then kneel, though from below, it looked like some stationary speck of cannon shot.

The wind and the effort of climbing intensified Pipistrello's blindness. His face showed exertion, the mouth opened, it was the head of a man climbing quickly as he can and on those features rode uncomfortably the shadows of the inactive eyes, a dark band that constantly attempted to right itself on the bridge of his nose. An odor of millet swept by; the earth tilted endlessly higher. Adeppi—there was a taste of blood in his throat from the climb—began to pull on the black sleeve.

"Pipistrello. Let us go back by the road."

Pipistrello only shrugged.

They ascended the sunlit mountain without turnstiles or wall and in the height loomed the impersonal wind, a faintly sweet-smelling vastness offering no protection.

Pipistrello laughed. "Porcellino, think of the dizziness of a fall from here, how the hands and heels of even a saint would roll!"

"Watch your step then. Cieco."

The summit rumbled. On the sunny slopes it was more audible, and for a moment, stopped still, they listened without feeling while the boulder turned its first few revolutions on the long way down. Gray, tombheavy, it came over the brink like a stone wheel. Adeppi saw it. Pipistrello heard and shook free of his guide.

The stone grew twice in girth while it was still far enough away to admire. It began to whistle as if there was a hole in its snout. Fifty ill-fitting church steps could be extracted from it. The hill, ever widening to the blue skies, now showed itself covered with stubble and impedimenta, and the boulder rose several feet into the air, thrown from its course and from the ground by the claw of a buried spring or head of turf. Again and again it leaped but returned to earth bearing upon them. And suddenly, dragging brambles and smaller stones, it was at hand.

"Which way? Which way, child?" screamed Pipistrello, too late.

Adeppi watched the white card of the sacred heart fluttering on the black half-twisted breast, still affixed though the blind man thrashed in his tracks. Until it vanished. There was a rush and it was past, that which shook the ground gone, leaving no trace. Already it was descended to the lower depths where there were only a few last trees to bar its flight.

Salve!

7

The tides are high at night and in the peak months of summer, and Adeppi finds they have risen in his absence to surpass the watermarks left the year before on the piles. The substructures have sunk and there is clear water atop dark. The stately gondolas are light, each occupied by a single pair who float behind drawn curtains smelling of seaweed. Half the city rides, having given no directions and at the mercy of gondoliers, burly men, masters of their decks, who now relax the oars. Adeppi need not ask them permission though as he jumps from prow to prow, one then another of these boatmen stops his oar entirely and peers at him through the darkness. He slips, one leg plunges into the water; there is laughter. Nearby the water has just climbed over the last step into a ballroom and spreads across the marble until it reaches the further wall. Ladies run lifting their grandaunts' embroidered skirts. A taper falls and splashes. But the musicians do not get wet, and the stranger water disturbs the festa only a moment. "Ancora, ancora," the boy dares to shout as he sees the men climb off their chairs and brave yellow stockings to the high tide.

A long gondola approaches from the opposite end of the city. He waits, then jumps, and rides once more past the palace where the lackeys, arm to arm, now drive against the rank few inches of sea their great brooms. And the water is rolled back so that up and down the canal a faint rocking possesses the dark flat-bottomed craft.

The totemic arms rising from the bows of the gondolas are striped around with bands of gilt and red paint, necks of the headless swans festooned by once rich color, pale and flaking as the groined vaults of a church with its peeling decoration and ancient quarrels. The gondolas have been hired for an evening on the lagoon bordered by apses and limpets dating centuries. Adeppi joins in the merriment and, for a night, is anonymous, as if he too is no more than a whelk glued among lichen and fern on the lower butts of a bridge, any moment in danger of being sheared away by an overly-anxious oar blade.

A gondola passes more severe in line than the rest. Its passenger, a priest, sits with curtains rolled tightly so that all may see he rides with his hands folded and alone. He tries to study the stone vines and inscriptions in the dark. He shouts, "Ferma!" But Adeppi's rower leans forward, without a command, and they are away.

Midnight is tolled by the collision of two of the pleasure boats. They ram, shake, list, and sink. A corked wine bottle and cushion rise from the debris and float toward the crevices where sewerage escapes between the stones. There is splashing as the parties attempt to disengage. Out of the lesser canals come continuous cries of warning, the "to the left," "to the right," and "sciar" of other gondoliers still moving without accident, close by. Up on the quai, those who have been saved from drowning begin their apologies. Even the boatmen are solicitous, panting for breath.

The city clears her tortuous channels, then once again they fill with the unlighted sweating flotilla that will lie becalmed by daybreak. A robbed man's pantaloons and ruffle are weighted, slipped over the side, and sunk. An old man, still pensioned to cry the time, peers cautiously down, spits into the water, and shakes his bell. Beyond the cathedral, the town house and chapel that rocks as a sea bell near the head of the lagoon, a silver porpoise is seen to approach and is driven off by the water rodents that swim knowingly at a depth just below the bottoms of the gondolas.

From three or four channels, late in the night, the city receives her indefatigable benediction and continues to slumber upon her fair winds and foul seas which in summer are high and pestiferous.

8

Some few days later Adeppi was caught by Gregorio Fabbisogno on the Via Saccheggio and beaten.

The coffin maker watched unmoved, not lowering his eyes until the whipping ended. It was dawn, the church nearby echoed with the exortation of the first mass chanted since sunrise, and the coffin maker, who had no taste for the sacrament, put on his spectacles the better to witness the punishment meted out not ten feet from him. The old man held his head before the scene with yellowed fixity—he was old but his temples were shaved high—until the expression changed and his mind carpentered some further death-like pleasure at the sight of the soldier struggling with the boy over a heap of dung. Fabbisogno could not have picked a better place than this—between the church covered like a lighthouse with the white of rooks and the shop hiding its row after row of incomplete coffins—to apostatize by the ministering of pain. Adeppi's shouts were a bridge in the silence from the misericordia to the Ancient paused now in the fashioning of caskets without a vow in his throat.

Gregario Fabbisogno beat the chrism into Adeppi's buttocks as if in a stupor, a soldier driven from his drunken, ill-pitched tent in the morning. The sight of a mad donkey—Mary had humbly ridden her—bloodied his eyes and he caught up the boy in his left arm. Cain was not more violent; with difficulty the coffin maker returned to his bony bench and nimbly squinted down the plank. And grimaced, noticing a curvature in that wooden spine. Those across the street had said barely fifty of the beads multiple as berries, and disappeared.

Only an hour before—it was the same moment that Dolce flung wide his shutters as he was bidden—Adeppi walked safely into the deserted haunt fronting the hospital and thought to beg breakfast from an old friend or his women. But the creche was no longer in its place and the small square, half in shadow, the upper half in new sunlight, was vacant, open to the sky. Vehicles, trucks, and motorcycles had decamped, hurrying southward in a retreat whose smoke still lingered above the smell of tires and gasoline siphoned into a knapsack.

One had been left behind. He seemed to lie in the surety that they would return for him. Adeppi recognized the litter and the water bottle at its side. Flat and deserted, the expanse of dust to the right and left, the body, though it was all that remained, shrank as he approached. The sun fell full in the darkened face. He lay an image of burned-out peace, all disaster come and gone. His thin form lay perpendicular to the steps and centered below the hospital doors which gaped as if they had just opened to eject him. Adeppi's footsteps did not startle the crossed arms. One trouser leg had been severed high as the belt, disclosing a knee and bones above and below which radiated the secret sun.

Adeppi stopped. But already, before he could turn and run, he was the discoverer of this stark, unmistakable survivor. The tops of the surrounding slanting roofs let through the light in irregular holes left by some olden, portentous damager; far below stood the bareheaded child, facing the prone creature that was diminished as a Bishop's sharp-chinned effigy atop his tomb. Now and then the boy heard a single unresolved musical note sounding over the still standing, brittle chimneys of his city. Lesser scratchings upon the air, the trickling from an upturned demijohn or the strangling of birds in the few overhead wires, were gone.

The hospital, its saline pits refilled with sand, offered an interior vacant as a routed, partially burned cathedral. It had long been inhabited, long abandoned, in front of it Adeppi would have removed his cap. But the way was blocked by the stranger on his back. Morning was the time for such a meeting, as the city was oldest after dawn. Here was a man, a treacherous curve to the claw and yellow upon the lips, in detail complete—thirteen ribs, a gray shirt, mouth open two fingers' width and in it, hardly visible, the tail end of a bandage. A body that grows heavier on the Italian slopes and is ringed round with bloody sticks.

At this hour Adeppi might have joined Urbino's younger children to kill carp in the canal. Instead: "Scusi. Come si chiama? Gianciotto? Gianni? Giovanni?" he asked. But immediately he became quiet.

About the stretcher was the odor of salt. The hospital was made of salt, the streets were white with salt, and Gianciotto, or perhaps Gianni, was tan on the belly and wrists where the garments had shrunk, a tan of the sea-shore, mountain, or still piazza that dressed the flesh and forced it back to the color of corrosion. The sea was still beyond the city walls. The body cast no shadow. Adeppi wanted to stay by it, guard it, yet the more he watched, the more he feared it. The inertness of an idle scythe in a field at the sea's edge, the formidableness of the body adrift, the look of the dead.

Adeppi backed to the stretcher, took hold of the handles, lifted and pulled. He began to sidestep, turn-ing it toward the shade. Ahead, he caught sight of a foul-smelling alcove and strained. In this country each of the fallen has a child to stumble upon him; from among the trees and irregular streets the boys call, waiting to hook themselves to those about to die. The stretcher resisted, shook, then slowly followed him, grating the dust and pebbles deposited Holy Year after Holy Year. It was not easy though the weight in its emollient costume yielded, and the boy grunted, hauled forward his wagon heaped with marrow and stones. The procession walked on little legs across the piazza. It was time for mass.

The exposed gray leg began to bend, wrinkling with the tension, the thin knee rose as if the sudden feeble onset of motion had loosed one last instinct under the bony cap. Adeppi continued to pull. Then the cleated military boot, belonging to some marching step of the past, drew back, shot up, and kicked the boy.

Adeppi did not turn, but as he escaped he loudly wailed: "Fratello mio, oh, fratello mio…disastro!"

The white donkey was tied before the church which in shape and ornamentation was a copy of the Basilica di S. Pietro. After a restless night and while its head hung stiffly in the halter, the donkey buried its character of servility in a noise that climbed high as the pinnacle. As the boy himself appeared within distance of the contracted nostrils and crooked ears, the beast became frenzied beyond control.

"Ahi, ahi!" shouted Gregario Fabbisogno and leapt from under the hooves.

Mary's small donkey lunged imprudently, lathering her white coat in ripples and bold waves down the narrow sides. She thrashed against the hunching figure of Fabbisogno who snatched now and then at the bridle, the wads of cloth wrapped around his bare feet paddling like the musty draggings of an executioner. Little of his face was visible, only the leathern elbows, the bandoleer, the arms shaking the chevrons up and down. A rider would sit this animal side saddle, face covered and holding limp hands in her lap. A pale pair, clicking safely along beneath the evergreens. She was thin, placid of gait, was protected from carrying loads heavier than the small woman who sat lightly near the rump. If Fabbisogno had confronted them, he would have lifted donkey, rider, and halo off the path in his two arms, cradling them, turned around and around, and shouted with rage.

The coffin maker, recognizing the cries of the donkey, came to his door and swept the shavings from a black apron. Then he watched, licking a finger he had crushed with a primitive rasp.

Adeppi, between man and donkey, cast up his round face to the frenzy of both. The animal beat her hooves and brayed when she seemed most out of breath, her stomach was loud and the very muscles added to the noise of each spasm.

There was blood on the backs of Fabbisogno's hands; he quailed, for at that moment he heard the woman behind him enter the Via Saccheggio and inquire after her mount, shook when he saw the donkey lift her nose and become calm. Adeppi stood up, surprised in the silence, and had time to notice the suspension of the dust they had driven into the sunlight. He saw the donkey nod her head as if about to drop it unconcernedly to the roughage trapped in the cobblestones—her eyes were turned from Fabbisogno. The three of them panted, Adeppi stared at the statuette of the donkey with drenched white coat, Fabbisogno crouched ready to fall upon the beast. The coffin maker cleared his throat.

"Ahi! Ahi! Ahi!"

Gregario Fabbisogno took one step, another, stooped

and quickly as possible pointed the rifle downward, holding it but a few inches from the white skull. He would
have wished to kill her in the stable of grace, perhaps as
she was reaching through the mild dusk for hay from a
crude rack, lightly flicking the hocks with the slender
tail. He would have wished to raise the rifle to his shoulder and destroy in a shot the peace of the animal among
her icons. He would mingle the smell of gunpowder
with her thorny dung and see her bump once, twice, to
the burnished planks and roll over.

Adeppi was cuffed to his knees and Fabbisogno's fist
began to rise and fall. It was open, sometimes closed, as
he beat he swung from side to side, abandon carrying
him in a slow dance. Fabbisogno thrashed him for the
donkey. The city roared at him and the boy more loud
than the rest. Gregario Fabbisogno sweated and peered
down the Via Saccheggio. But suddenly he stopped,
swayed, and sat back. He loosed his arms and Adeppi
rolled from him.

They emerged softly into the sunlight after mass: the
masons to the endless reconstruction of Il Duomo, the
clerks to their courts, a few loiterers to the benches above
the sewers. And with them, lastly, came Dolce who had
just given up this town's unfamiliar censer to its bag of
ashes.

Dolce did not hesitate. He approached and laid his
hand on Gregario Fabbisogno's head. He waited and,
as the man remained dumb, gently shook him by the
hair. When the carabiniere opened his eyes, Dolce
stooped and made the sign. Once more, swiftly, with

slight affection, so that he might comprehend. And the priest allowed the black eyes to close again.

Without even this formality Dolce took Adeppi by the hand and led him away, avoiding the donkey and the crowd.

The body before the hospital had disappeared.

Up and down the Via Saccheggio sounded the drudgery of the crooked hammer and crooked nails.

Palms

Two fat coadjutors and a thin—Dolce, Brother Bolo, and a lay brother—do not allow their asses a moment's lag but ride them without relaxing the rein and watch the rocks slipping underfoot, the gallows approach and pass. Brother Bolo has a red face and thick brown hair that shines with the paternosters of his seclusion; he travels balancing a heavy stone upon the low center of his donkey's spine. Dolce is empty handed, mendicant; the elderly woman rides with him. The three are followed by a wing of yellow bees that answer roughly in the heat.

The graces' donkeys look as if they have just been beaten from the bushes and appear quickly, hard driven, round every turn in the road, baleful under Thomist ejaculations. Dolce's mount, the smallest of the three, trips now and then, having been lame as long as he can remember. The woman's feet are uncovered; he holds her waist. Brother Bolo and Dolce abreast grunt to the jogging of the animals. The lay brother trails silently. The trio wear black smocks upon which are painted rough white stripes, bones, false ribs. They pass a tall water wheel turned only by the wind, and from its dark buckets peer the bodies of children wrapped in vines.

Gray dogs come out from their dens, from under haystacks, from white abbey and villages, to sniff silently their train. The religious travel more slowly now and Dolce clutches the woman tightly lest she be snatched away. Watchers along the way wait to proffer stumps of candles, toss handfuls of eye teeth in their path.

In their arms, against their bellies, the women with sores carry sacks of flour that have been dropped for them. The clothing is torn from their bodies wherever the scabs lie, no matter on which limb or whether front or back. The abrasions, each time verified with a kiss, long judged unremediable and painful, are exhibited noiselessly and listlessly. She there, studying her fallen hands, bore a dog with a torch in his mouth; behind her, a girl canonized at the age of seven. Even the tooth-less have the sweet smiles of the beatified. In the enclo-sure of the nunnery, matrons wearing white Flemish caps urge them aside for the entrance of the donkeys.

Dolce and Brother Bolo present themselves at the gate. The nuns do not rise. They continue on their knees, working up and down the corridors, pulling the iron pails, and the Prioress too bends across her brush. The donkey bearing the woman is led into their slippery cloister, onto their white stones. Spread eagle in each tall window is a black angel. The donkey drinks from one of the pails, then lifts its head and smells the smoke in the court.

Beyond the nuns, in a small grill-covered space, a young girl, flapping her sackcloth apron, tends the fire. She is the only woman inside the convent on her feet. She does not pray and sleeps under a half roof against the wood, her legs toward the pyre. Her arms and hands are blistered and her face marked with soot. Dolce pushes the white donkey close to the flames. The girl does not look up at once but pokes and digs at the fire which leaps above her head and reddens the coarse rods in the grill.

Bolo assists him, but the girl is strong and swings the burden to her shoulder and from the shoulder off, away with one sweep as the religious beat the sudden firebrands off their skirts. It is done. Theresa, Adeppi's mother, goes headlong into the pile, breaks through the red perishable tangle of illuminated twigs, falls to the live coals in the center—to flame her stocking, bodice, and shawl.

The smoke suddenly grows thick.

Three days Dolce prayed for him. The boy stood in a corner, without clothes, turned toward the wall so that he might see. At times it appeared that Dolce was not speaking on his behalf at all. Nor did the priest speak to the boy. Now and then Adeppi tried tapping on the wall, thinking that someone might hear him. In a fashion he too was praying.

The priest, unquenchable, wore a white shirt and thought sanctus, sanctus, sanctus for the benefit of the flesh hardly more than infant. The shutters were fast. Adeppi spent the hours watching the inhuman descent of a small red spider riding its loose intimate strand of web late in the oppressive afternoons.

The more fervently Dolce prayed, the hotter it grew. He seemed to have at hand an immeasurable rote of pious negatives that applied endlessly to the narrow shoulders before him. He would not sit, but in the heat that rolled over the city stood firm, a figure of black and ivory marching behind the naked boy through many entrances to absolution. Hat off, neck bare, no blessed medallion in sight, Dolce challenged the transgression of the child.

Dolce had not raised his voice, but it became faint. Now and then, at any moment and with no anticipation in the rest of his body, he would fling out his arms and allow St. Elmo's fire to dance from his fingertips.

Fabbisogno lay drunk below by the bar. "Vino, vino," he ordered but no one served him.

Adeppi had not known there were so many saints. As Dolce prayed, the boy saw them, their stooping bodies moving before the façade of a black cathedral. The Pontiff's thousand eyes looked sharp. For the last hours the spider refused to descend the thread, hovering above in its knotted nest. Dolce whispered. The severe neckline of the white shirt, the eyeballs, white, round, the black wrap of the lower garment, all things soft, soluble, transient, and dusty. His cuffs were frayed. He bowed his head and in shadow and under the sharp nose hid the movement of lips and gullet, losing sight of the boy.

While offering a prayer aloud to St. Francis, he fell into a pale sleep on the third night. Conscious that he was allowing the boy a chance to escape, he tried calling out. Then he dreamed of a traveler and companion he had seen at the gates of Vatican City, the dissolute wearing a straw hat with a red band and in the sun, amidst the sober and sick, a suit of large checks; the other, with a great head of black hair, was using his shoulder against those who pressed near. The two slowly followed through the crowd a small bare-backed boy whom they urged to wail melodiously and beg. They were purporting to bring him, in a moment or two, before His Holiness. The crowd was diverted at the very threshold of the Sanctum and the most impoverished of them, those hunched on rude litters, were seduced into a laugh. Dolce groaned. The walls of the Vatican were whispering and in the distance he saw the popedom slowly recoil, forever beyond reach, close with the steady precision of an enormous flower rejecting the dark.

He fell to his knees. Several in the crowd began to dance. Past his eye went the twisting heels. One dropped a piece of spiced meat under his nose. To his helplessness there came the persistent secular singing of the boy. Suddenly there was a tugging at his back. "Pray for me, Padre?" whispered the singer himself, "pray for me?"

Dolce woke. He was lying with his face toward the ceiling, hands far flung, and his feet dragged partly off the bed; the bottom of his robe had risen and when he lifted his head he saw his legs, silhouetted, the many times mended black shoes sticking up and old, pinched. His head ached and he was unable to move. As he gathered himself, the door opened.

Edouard rocked back and forth holding the edge of it. The light came in over his shoulder, unwavering. The front of his nightcoat was blotched and one of the flies remained with him, spreading its blue wings to his death. Edouard peered in a moment too long from the threshold. With effort he lifted a hand to his hips—but he was about to fall—and stared into the disordered room. The veins had burst under his eyes, there was a disused black sling hanging from his neck, the cold fingers could be seen feeling his heart.

Then he lifted his chin, managed an old look of affection, laughed and reeled back, saying, "Scusi, scusi," trying to wink. But he was not able to pull the door closed after him.

Dolce ran into the hall. He stood listening with his hand to his ear and his stomach suddenly clenched in hunger. There, he took a step, there it was again, the dying man was whistling to himself. Then he sniffed, looked down, and discovered the boy at his side.

9

So Edouard lay back upon the coverlet. His straw hat tilted from the bedpost. Somewhere, within the yellow of his memory, he heard an old woman snipping branches with an iron shears. Once, from a third-class compartment, he had seen a village with imbricated tiles the color of rouge, and against a wall in the sunlight a young priest who hardly lifted his eyes to watch the train, the priest concentrating upon a toy, a game he held in his two hands, turning it that way and another way, shaking it, trying to replace the whiskers on the cat. Perhaps the cat still had no whiskers, this not having been accomplished in all of Edouard's lifetime. And yet he could not help thinking that they should have patience, and he hoped the priest had not moved a step beyond his village.

Edouard folded his hands across his breast. One leg

slipped from the coverlet and hung irretrievably off the bed. He thought he heard the grating of death's gate, the plash of the oar, but nevertheless had hopes for himself. It was the survival of the least fit; and though he was denied a sight of Il Duomo, he recalled the endless columns of old women and boys passing one to the next the bricks and piling them. They would not let him go too soon, for decade after decade only those who were thin survived, all who remained thus faring on one less green leaf, on water the more impure. And the rivers crept across Lombardy and covered the toes of the dead.

The Sforza family was all but dead. The egg scavengers walked across the field at dusk. All but dead, but not dead for there was always one more who lived like a mythical monster in the maremma. And Edouard thought of the centuries to come with a drop of blood shared by a hundred, and the generations it would take for the sports to appear, when men would be dwarfed and withered of limb, when the weak, the sickest, and the abandoned would steal the figs from the archbishop's tree and inherit the plains wherever the wind blew.

He looked down at himself and thought, "How many bellies such as this one, how many legs like these, how many bones and ligatures like those cannot die. How many are wearing my coat tonight?" Gene after gene was untrue, trait after trait ill-advised, and there remained the intemperate, starving, treacherous, cold demeanor of those who could not be trusted into limbo. And he would not have changed the tide at night, nor halted its backflowing. His own life now depended upon listening, upon hearing the coming of discomfort, day-dreaming of uncharitable children. No, they could not afford to lose Edouard. And he smiled, thinking of the slow retraction of heat and light—in each of them—making the blood bad that the tall grass of the maremma and the dust of the cities might surfeit them. It was peaceful to return, to ask of the crows where the men were and be told and to climb the hill and find them.

Who was there to despair for Jacopo? Who was there to despair for himself? "Bene." He could not roll over. The Grand Hotel was burning.

It rained. The hills washed down into the groves and the clay ran white. A sluggish rain slid from the backs of the buildings, the water rose and drowned the reeds in the marsh. By morning the cobblestones were finally clean.

"Signore," Adeppi rubbed his eyes and inquired of a stranger, "what day is it? If you please, Signore." The man caught him by the hand and led him through the Bocca di Piazza, under the arch, down the steep and past the well yard to the edge of the city. There a crowd was gathered at the foot of a hill, pressed far as possible from the last segments of the wall. The rain came down as a cup spilling. It was early, before the matins, and lightning bolted swiftly over their heads through the gray cloud, seeking its ground. Adeppi pushed among the popolari, clawing at a woman's cloak.

The field was soft, rangeless, clay, he could not see its boundaries where it sank into the fog. Behind them were the forgotten chains and the emptiness of the Via Tozzo. The alarm had spread among them and they had come to the open, into the rain and under the natural electric startling of the heaven. Dolce stood a few feet in front of the crowd, behind him they awaited his sign. Over the hills in the aqueduct the rats lay down stealthily until the way should be clear again.

Dolce took the censer proffered him and began to swing it, dull and silver, smoking to the right, to the left, sounding as the swing of a gate, this ritual performed at the edge of the bare field to protect them so that they put their hands upon their breasts. Dolce fed it the beating of his heart.

"Patience, patience, temperance, patience," said Dolce. Firmly with the other hand he took hold of Adeppi's shoulder, all the while swinging, smoking, watching.

The eyes were upon the body in the clay beyond them. Only Adeppi glanced up to see the crow flying. The silent figure turned in the white mud. Dragging itself, slowly animated, hardly visible, bones of the fingers resting upon the rot of the helmet filled with mud, its bare head lifted and was unable to catch breath in the rain.

He ran, darted, and sank suddenly into the beginning of the plain upon which no city could be built, sloughing through the forgotten furrows, against the restraining priest and crowd behind him. The moment passed and their breaths were no longer at his neck. The boy raced and the body in the field flung up his head. The priest held back the crowd, with his arms wide stopped them, but he could not stop their cry. "O sacrilegio, sacrilegio!"

The earth was cold.

At the breaking of that day, high in the mountains, Nino huddled with his head biting the crossed arms and lay close to the earth chopped from the entrenchments in the black cliff, Nino cold, bearded, and deaf to the turn of the world drifting up from the sea below. The wind touched the hair and pulled listlessly at the great-coat upon his back, but disturbed him not as did not the howl of the sentries and the gulls. Under his hands, behind the face, deep inside the dark sac of the brain, he dreamed of them and it persisted, a continuous dream, warm and without waiting and despite the presence across the valley of the enemy.

JOHN HAWKES

John Hawkes was born in 1925 in Stamford, Connecticut. He is the author of over fourteen novels, several of them drawn from his experiences and travels, which include a youth in Juneau, Alaska and New York City and his World War II service as an ambulance driver for the American Field Service in Italy and Germany.

His first book, published in 1949, was *The Cannibal*, a short novel about a neo-Nazi uprising in an imaginary Germany, which attracted critical attention. *The Bettle Leg*, Hawkes's "surrealist Western" followed in 1951. In 1954 he published two short novels in one volume, *The Goose on the Grave* AND *The Owl* (reprinted here as *The Owl* AND *The Goose on the Grave)*, which further established his reputation. A series of three novels, *The Lime Twig* (1961), *Second Skin* (1964), and *The Blood Oranges* (1971) catapulted him to the forefront of American letters.

Since 1971, he has published, to continued acclaim, *Death, Sleep & The Traveler* (1974), *Travesty* (1976), *The Passion Artist* (1979), *Virginie* (1982), *Adventures in the Alaskan Skin Trade* (1985), *Innocence in Extremis* (1985), and *Whistlejacket* (1988). His most recent work is *Sweet William: a Memoir of Old Horse.*

He is a member of the American Academy of Arts and Letters, and currently lives in Providence, Rhode Island, where he taught many years as a professor at Brown University.

SUN & MOON CLASSICS

This publication was made possible, in part, through an operational grant from the Andrew W. Mellon Foundation and through contributions from the following individuals:

Charles Altieri (Seattle, Washington)
John Arden (Galway, Ireland)
Paul Auster (Brooklyn, New York)
Jesse Huntley Ausubel (New York, New York)
Dennis Barone (West Hartford, Connecticut)
Jonathan Baumbach (Brooklyn, New York)
Guy Bennett (Los Angeles, California)
Bill Berkson (Bolinas, California)
Steve Benson (Berkeley, California)
Charles Bernstein and Susan Bee (New York, New York)
Dorothy Bilik (Silver Spring, Maryland)
Alain Bosquet (Paris, France)
In Memoriam: John Cage
In Memoriam: Camilo José Cela
Bill Corbett (Boston, Massachusetts)
Fielding Dawson (New York, New York)
Robert Crosson (Los Angeles, California)
Tina Darragh and P. Inman (Greenbelt, Maryland)
Christopher Dewdney (Toronto, Canada)
Arkadii Dragomoschenko (St. Petersburg, Russia)
George Economou (Norman, Oklahoma)
Kenward Elmslie (Calais, Vermont)
Elaine Equi and Jerome Sala (New York, New York)
Lawrence Ferlinghetti (San Francisco, California)
Richard Foreman (New York, New York)
Howard N. Fox (Los Angeles, California)
Jerry Fox (Aventura, Florida)
In Memoriam: Rose Fox
Melvyn Freilicher (San Diego, California)
Miro Gavran (Zagreb, Croatia)
Allen Ginsberg (New York, New York)
Peter Glassgold (Brooklyn, New York)
Barbara Guest (New York, New York)

Perla and Amiram V. Karney (Bel Air, California)
Fred Haines (Los Angeles, California)
Václav Havel (Prague, The Czech Republic)
Lyn Hejinian (Berkeley, California)
Fanny Howe (La Jolla, California)
Harold Jaffe (San Diego, California)
Ira S. Jaffe (Albuquerque, New Mexico)
Pierre Joris (Albany, New York)
Alex Katz (New York, New York)
Tom LaFarge (New York, New York)
Mary Jane Lafferty (Los Angeles, California)
Michael Lally (Santa Monica, California)
Norman Lavers (Jonesboro, Arkansas)
Jerome Lawrence (Malibu, California)
Stacey Levine (Seattle, Washington)
Herbert Lust (Greenwich, Connecticut)
Norman MacAffee (New York, New York)
Rosemary Macchiavelli (Washington, DC)
Beatrice Manley (Los Angeles, California)
In Memoriam: Mary McCarthy
Harry Mulisch (Amsterdam, The Netherlands)
Iris Murdoch (Oxford, England)
Martin Nakell (Los Angeles, California)
In Memoriam: bpNichol
Toby Olson (Philadelphia, Pennsylvania)
Maggie O'Sullivan (Hebden Bridge, England)
Rochelle Owens (Norman, Oklahoma)
Marjorie and Joseph Perloff (Pacific Palisades, California)
Dennis Phillips (Los Angeles, California)
Carl Rakosi (San Francisco, California)
Tom Raworth (Cambridge, England)
David Reed (New York, New York)
Ishmael Reed (Oakland, California)
Janet Rodney (Santa Fe, New Mexico)
Joe Ross (Washington, DC)
Jerome and Diane Rothenberg (Encinitas, California)
Dr. Marvin and Ruth Sackner (Miami Beach, Florida)
Floyd Salas (Berkeley, California)
Tom Savage (New York, New York)
Leslie Scalapino (Oakland, California)
James Sherry (New York, New York)

Aaron Shurin (San Francisco, California)
Charles Simic (Strafford, New Hampshire)
Gilbert Sorrentino (Stanford, California)
Catharine R. Stimpson (Staten Island, New York)
John Taggart (Newburg, Pennsylvania)
Nathaniel Tarn (Tesuque, New Mexico)
Fiona Templeton (New York, New York)
Mitch Tuchman (Los Angeles, California)
Hannah Walker and Ceacil Eisner (Orlando, Florida)
Wendy Walker (New York, New York)
Anne Walter (Carnac, France)
Jeffery Weinstein (New York, New York)
Mac Wellman (Brooklyn, New York)
Arnold Wesker (Hay on Wye, England)

If you would like to be a contributor to this series, please send your tax-deductible contribution to The Contemporary Arts Educational Project, Inc., a non-profit corporation, 6026 Wilshire Boulevard, Los Angeles, California 90036.

SUN & MOON CLASSICS

Author	Title
Alferi, Pierre	*Natural Gait* 95 ($10.95)
Antin, David	*Selected Poems: 1963–1973* 10 ($12.95)
Barnes, Djuna	*At the Roots of the Stars: The Short Plays* 53 ($12.95)
	The Book of Repulsive Women 59 ($6.95)
	Interviews 86 ($13.95)
	New York 5 ($12.95)
	Smoke and Other Early Stories 2 ($10.95)
Bernstein, Charles	*Content's Dream: Essays 1975–1984* 49 ($14.95)
	Dark City 48 ($11.95)
	Rough Trades 14 ($10.95)
Bjorneboe, Jens	*The Bird Lovers* 43 ($9.95)
Breton, André	*Arcanum 17* 51 ($12.95)
	Earthlight 26 ($12.95)
Bromige, David	*The Harbormaster of Hong Kong* 32 ($10.95)
Butts, Mary	*Scenes from the Life of Cleopatra* 72 ($13.95)
Cadiot, Olivier	*L'Art Poétique* 98 ($10.95)
Celan, Paul	*Breathturn* 74 ($12.95)
Coolidge, Clark	*The Crystal Text* 99 ($11.95)
	Own Face 39 ($10.95)
	The Rova Improvisations 34 ($11.95)
Copioli, Rosita	*The Blazing Lights of the Sun* 84 ($11.95)
de Nerval, Gérard	*Aurélia* 103 ($12.95)
De Angelis, Milo	*Finite Intuition* 65 ($11.95)
DiPalma, Ray	*Numbers and Tempers: Selected Early Poems* 24 (11.95)